James,

I hope you enjoy my magical world of Reelsville as much as I enjoyed writing it!

Warmest Regards,

AN AWAKENING

WENDY M. KOK

ISBN: 978-1-66780-510-8 (print)
ISBN: 978-1-66780-511-5 (ebook)

CONTENTS

So now faith, hope, and love abide, these three;

But the greatest of these is love.

1 Corinthians 13:13

THE OAKLEY ~ DECEMBER 1968

Brooke

I lean my head against the window of Kelly's car. We're both buzzing from a day of shopping, and laughter comes easy as I feel the summer breeze flowing through my hair. It's warm but not too hot, it's one of those days where the temperature sits at a perfect seventy-six degrees and everything feels effortless. Like everyone has taken their happy pills and empathy is personified.

I wish I had the ability to bottle up these days. I would keep them hidden away in a drawer, referring back to them when I needed to. Something to hold on to, when life starts to turn sour.

We extended our excursion with an early dinner at Diablo Café. We happened upon this place by accident and were able to score a corner booth with the most perfect view of the most famous bridge in the area, the Oakley. The bridge runs over the river, and at this hour, is jammed packed with traffic. We were stuck behind it not too long ago, and my stomach is grateful for the reprieve.

I sip the last of my margarita, licking the salt off the rim —the best part of the drink, if you ask me—and reach for a final chip, using it to scoop the last of the guacamole into my mouth. The guacamole here is superb. Successful Mexican restaurants always know how to make a good guac.

I glance out the floor-to-ceiling windows. The sun is low enough in the sky now that the lights of the Oakley start flickering on, washing everything surrounding it in a golden honey hue.

We're in the car minutes later and back on the bridge, which is still packed. As we move at a snail's pace forward, I start to feel an impressive jab at my chest.

That's what I get for ordering a burrito the size of a dinner plate.

Riding over bridges is something I don't like to do, and I feel that same way about heights. Both wake things up in me that I don't care to feel.

There is some sort of commotion ahead of us, our windows are rolled down, and I can hear arguments in the air. I gather from bits and pieces of the conversation, that someone has been rear-ended.

From the driver's seat, Kelly leans as far out the window as she can. She surveys the scene and scrunches up her nose. "Someone's not happy up there."

My heart starts to race, but I reassure myself that this is just a little snag. *We'll get off the bridge soon enough.*

"Always someone driving crazy on this thing," she mutters, turning up the radio. She's well aware of my aversion to bridges.

A familiar song comes on the radio, but the upbeat lyric does little to settle my nerves.

"I love this song," Kelly says, singing along with the next line.

Despite the happy tune, I can't shake off the heaviness around me. There's unease and frustration swirling about, and at first, I think it's because of the fender bender ahead of us.

It's more than that though, like some impending doom lurking around the corner.

I know these feelings. They sure aren't pleasant, but ignoring them makes it worse.

I hear the squaw of a large crow perched high in the tree that borders the bridge. He's looking down at all of us—we probably look quite small to him. I watch as he tilts his head this way and that, making me think he's privy to information that I don't have.

This kind of knowledge is only reserved for us birds.

The ground beneath me shifts, and my stomach shifts with it. A sharp, screeching rings out, and metallic groans pierce the evening air as we start shaking—me, the car, Kelly, even the vehicles around us and the people standing outside. *It feels like the whole world is shaking.*

The crow is still eyeing us, watching as the bridge lets out an annoyed sigh at the top of its lungs.

Kelly's wide eyes catch mine.

"What's going on?" I'm quite certain that I don't want to know. The color of Kelly's face goes from toasty suntan to whitish grey. That's what scares me the most: how quickly she turned into a ghost. And that's when I ask the most obvious question.

"What's wrong?"

Like she knows. All I have to do is look around us—everything is wrong. Wrong is all around us, paying us a little visit.

"Oh God . . . the bridge," I croak out, unable to move as my worst fears are realized.

Huge pieces of cement are falling all around us, and I'm stuck in this seat.

Do I get up and leave, or stay?

I can't think. I grab onto whatever I can, which is the handle of the glove compartment, of all things. The swaying bridge beneath us gives the sensation that I am sitting on a swing, enjoying a summer's day, and for a few seconds, I believe it.

I catch the last few seconds of a jagged piece of concrete as it falls on someone standing right in front of our car. It catches the lower part of his legs, and he's screaming. There's so much noise around us, I can't even hear him now—I just watch as he opens his mouth, but it's like his voice is on mute.

I'm struck at how quickly things have escalated in a matter of minutes.

"We've gotta get out of here!" Kelly yells, reaching for her seatbelt.

I glance out the rear window and see a path back to land, back to safety and normalcy. It's not that far away, and yet, I still can't seem to move. The path is still intact, but it won't be for long. Kelly screams as another piece of cement lands a few feet from her door. "Oh my God!"

I stare as people scramble and sprint, leaping from their cars and running past ours. I see that Kelly has gotten out of ours.

"Come on!" she screeches through the still-open door. There's a hysterical urgency to her voice. I'll always remember it.

But I can't move. I can't get any part of my body except my head to move—all I can do is watch. I glance down at the water below. Cement pieces are still falling, a raining cascade of powdery grey.

The car rolls forward, and I suck in a breath. I'm still in this car. And I have no hopes of stopping it. And in that moment, I know were about to hit water.

Next stop, the lake.

The Oakley, once massive and majestic, in a matter of seconds, has been reduced to crumbling pieces of cement soup, all of it pouring into the lake.

This is not a bridge anymore.

I turn around just in time to catch the last glimpse of my friend, waving her hands like a maniac. It would be almost funny, if this was just a dream. But it's not.

The car is rolling off what's left of the bridge now, with me, right along with it.

The water hits with such force, I'm thrown into the windshield. I think my jaw might have hit the glove compartment. I notice an immediate pain penetrating the side of my face, and I feel a wave of regret that I didn't get out. And then, well . . .

I don't know what happens next.

$$\smile$$

Am I dead?

It kinda feels that way. My first coherent thought is hazy. My head is throbbing.

I want to open my eyes, but they feel like weights are on them. I keep trying anyway. Waking up seems impossible, and my brain feels foggy. Everything feels heavy, and I want to just lie here and sleep. And yet, something inside of me wants me to wake.

I feel like I'm trying to crawl my way out of a tunnel of clear jello.

What is it about trippy dreams? What does trippy even mean anyway? I can't even tell you. I've never gotten high. Not yet anyway— inhaling smoke never appealed to me. You can thank my parents for that . . . try eating dinner when they're smoking like chimneys two feet away at the dinner table . . .

As the jello sensation leaves, it is replaced by a ringing, and my ears feel like they're on fire. *A busted ear drum, perhaps?*

How long was I out? Seconds?

I take in what's in front of me, and it doesn't look good. I was out long enough for me and the car to sink to the bottom of the lake.

I have to get out of this car.

I'm underwater, but there doesn't appear to be any water inside, not yet, anyway. I look around, wondering why.

Maybe I hit an air pocket.

I feel an annoying drip hit my eye. At first I think it's the water coming in, but when I bring my hand up, I realize it's my own blood. It's sticky, and there's a copper tanginess in the air. I wonder where else I might be bleeding from, but that's the least of my problems. I have to get out of here, and to do that, I have to see.

I swipe at my eyes, transferring most of the blood to my sleeve. My heart rate starts to pick up. Any minute now I'm expecting water to come gushing in.

I try the door handle, but it doesn't budge. I glance out the window, spying eerie shapes of cars in the water with me, and I catch one still making its way down. I feel bad for whoever is in that car.

Hey there, genius. You're in the same position.

Even though it's murky and dark, I can still sense movement inside the car in front of me. And in a sick way, it feels nice to know that I'm not alone.

I know, it's selfish.

Two more cars make their way down, headlights on high beam. The lights ensure we can see everything down here with us at the bottom of the lake. And everything around here feels like a watery grave.

Something strange floats past my window—it looks like a package. I find it hard to believe that something like this is floating on past, still wrapped up in green paper, a trail of red ribbon floating behind. *A floating present.*

I remember then that Christmas is in five days, and I still haven't finished my shopping. Now, I never will.

The realization that I will probably drown down here is sinking in. I almost laugh—in any other situation, I would find it rather comical that I chose the word *sink*. But instead, my heart races, my breathing speeds up, and I try to choke the panic down.

At the same time, I see an outline of someone swimming. He's heading right for my car—well, Kelly's car, I should say. I wonder if he's an angel. I sure hope so—I sure could use one.

I feel a small glimmer of hope as he peers in. His short brown hair flows lazily in the water.

He has kind eyes.

He points at the door repeatedly, waking me up from my shock. I mouth the words "It won't open," and he motions for me to move over to the driver side, which I do.

I expect that any minute now he'll be swimming away. A person can only hold their breath for so long. I yell the words "Just go!" knowing he can't hear me, but I have to try. I point my finger upward, over and over again, willing him to safety. *Save yourself.*

He keeps shaking his head.

But then he swims away, and I can't see him anymore. *Good,* I think, *that's what you should do.* Though some part of me still wishes he'd stayed.

I then see him swim back, and this time there's a piece of driftwood in his hand.

Oh, good Lord in heaven, he's going to try to break the window.

I've taken enough science classes to know that this is not going to work—there's too much pressure down here. Why doesn't he just leave this horrible place?

We exchange a look, and there is this, well, *knowing* . . . I see it in his eyes. But he still tries banging on the door, which still doesn't open. *What now?*

I can't look at him anymore—it's too painful. If he is going to swim up to the surface—which I know at any moment he will—I don't want to know when.

So, I close my eyes, I pretend I'm somewhere else, but the beautiful stranger never leaves my thoughts. *Swim away from here,* I silently plead. *There's nothing down here but death.*

Water is trickling in now at a steady pace. There's about an inch of it on the floorboards already, and I can feel its squishy iciness inside my sneakers. I glance down at my shoes—they're my favorite ones, Black Converse. I pull my feet up, tucking them underneath me on the seat. I can feel the fear now—it runs through me like a hot poker. But along with this fear, is the strange feeling of warmth, and I look over out the window.

He's still here!

His eyes are the brightest blue. My heart squeezes just staring into them, they're all I want to look at. Their light so vastly different from the putrid darkness of the lake.

The lake of death.

His eyes are a promise to me, a promise of everything that is good in the world. A promise of compassion, hope. Faith and stability. A promise of things to come, both now and in the future.

His eyes promise love.

And love is eternal.

I love him so much for that, for just being there. But can a person really love someone they don't even know?

Sure, they can.

There isn't much left to do, so I pray. I pray that despite the odds, we will get another chance to meet. And that when we do, there will be an unexplained *knowing*—like two people who have found their missing parts.

I always thought the notion of reincarnation was an interesting one; I sure hope it is true.

That's the last thought I have, before I die.

ETHEL'S FUNERAL

Brooke

I'm standing in a sea of umbrellas. The rain isn't letting up, and as much as I want to pay my respects to Ethel, I find it difficult to be here. Neelson's funeral home has seen a steady rise in their business, and I'm powerless to do anything about it. I'm still human after all, my listening powers have long since gone.

But because of that, I now feel powerless to anything malevolent that might be coming my way. This heavy uneasiness, my constant companion these days, makes me want to jump out of my own skin. I can't do anything I want to do, and it's driving me crazy.

So, I lie. I pretend that this whole sham of a funeral is real, and that Ethel drowned. Even though that's most definitely **not** what happened.

I close my eyes and try to remember how Ethel used to be. But no matter how hard I try, older images of her just won't come. I can only see the twisted version of her—the demon trying to claw its way into me and my friends. Any human image of Ethel has been wiped clean by the memory of that dark night.

Cassie is standing across from me. Her face is hidden, half by an umbrella, the other half by all her makeup. There's a young woman standing next to her, and I'm still waiting for the introductions. Cassie appears to be shaking non-stop, either from the cold or from her own emotions. But either way, she's looking like she's one step away from a Vesuvius-level outburst.

As soon as the minister finishes the service and moves to offer her his condolences, Cassie's voice reaches my ears over the steady din of the rain. "Oh, dear heaven on earth, I must look a complete fright."

I try not to roll my eyes as the minister says a few last words before heading out to his car. Cassie's idea of a "fright" is leaving the house without pantyhose or mascara—hardly a reason for her theatrics, but then again, she's never needed one. Even today, she's outdressed us all with her smart-fitting suit, ruby-red lips, and perfectly coiffed hair that wraps around her head like a cinnamon bun. Princess Leia, eat your heart out.

She was crying during most of the service, her dark trails of mascara trickling down like a muddy waterfall. But she still managed to look glamorous. I watched as she dabbed at her eyes every few seconds with her perfect, linen handkerchief.

After another elegant and poised dab under her eyes, she looks over at me, her lips churning into a frown. I know what she's about to say, and I brace myself for her words.

She raises her voice to be heard over the rain. "Brooke, would it kill you to put on some lipstick?"

I stop myself from shaking my head. I'd hoped maybe she would have thought of something a little more profound—this is her best friend's funeral, after all. But I should know by now that Cassie and substance often don't mix.

I hear murmurs beside me, and sense an uneasy shuffling as the other attendees—who'd clearly heard her comment—shifted from one foot to the other.

Cassie thrives on creating a scene. And she will never understand that I would rather spend money on a box of night crawlers than on a tube of lipstick. But I will gladly discuss lipstick shades with her instead of the real reason we all were here.

It's hard to get the last image of Ethel out of my mind. She was in a zombie-like state, crawling out of the lake like some animal, her dark hair clinging to her back like moving snakes. Funny, when she was a regular human, her hair was never that color or that long.

That fact only upped the creep factor and made me realize the drastic lengths these things would go to in an attempt to trick people.

Sometimes I dream of her, and it's always the same. Ethel clawing her way out of the grave, wearing nothing but a simple, white night-gown. There's mud splattered all over it, and I can see it oozing between her fingers as she makes her way out. She then asks us if we would like more of her potato salad.

I don't think I'll ever eat potato salad again.

A chill runs through me as I worry for Cassie. She's a tough old broad for sure, but everyone has their breaking point.

It's still raining as we head to our cars, and I'm grateful the funeral home planned a dinner in the large banquet hall nearby. I long to be out of this rain, into some warmth, and away from Cassie's big mouth.

Lyle is here, of course, his eyes showing the beginnings of a pie-eyed buzz. In another hour, the end of his nose will start looking like a piece of cauliflower.

Ethel didn't have a husband at the time or much family that I knew of, but there are mumblings of a nephew who might be in attendance.

I glance around the banquet hall to see if I can find him. When I spy a lone man sitting by himself at a table, I put two and two together. His eyes dart around like he wants to be elsewhere.

The funny thing about funerals is their potential to bring people together. The people that want to be brought together, at least. A proverbial shot of adrenaline to relationships that might have gone stale.

I notice that the doctor from the med center is here, that's strange. He's a new resident in town, according to the Neelsville gossip. Maybe since Ethel had been such a stable fixture in Neelsville, he might have felt an obligation to pay his respects.

I stifle a groan as Cassie heads my way. I'm still waiting for Cassie to introduce me to the girl she's dragging along with her.

"Seems I forgot my manners outside, dear. Brooke, this is my niece, Scout."

I give her an amiable smile as we fall into step next to each other, circling the room.

"Hi."

Scout's wearing a long-sleeved shirt with the word "Pepsi" scrolled on the front. An interesting choice for a funeral, but, so be it. Her hair is styled like Farrah Fawcett and despite the éléments, looks downright fantastic.

"What do you guys do for fun around here?"

She's looking for fun at a funeral?

I couldn't help but frown at her statement. Noticing my obvious distaste, she explains.

"Sorry, but I never met Ethel. They made me come here."

Cassie drops her gaze and leans in. "Now, Scout, be decent."

I watch as Cassie trips on a piece of uneven linoleum, breaking off a piece of her heel.

"Oh, Christ, my shoe!"

Her voice rings out into the air as we jerk to a stop beside her.

She bends down, attempting to put the heel back on, but the damage is done. The shoe is a goner.

"Ethel never did like these shoes. You think it's a sign?" she muses, her eyes shooting toward the high ceiling.

Over the last few days, whenever something unusual happened, Cassie would think it's a sign. If a bird took a dump on her head, she would think it was a sign from Ethel, her last and final "eff you" to her friend.

"Oh, Ethel!" With that, Cassie starts in again with the crying, pulling out yet another fresh handkerchief out of her handbag. It appears she has an endless supply.

After dabbing her eyes while making an exaggerated "O" with her mouth, I see her eyes catch on someone across the room. She sniffles dramatically. "Excuse me, but I think Lyle needs some tending."

As soon as Cassie walks away, Scout starts talking. "I can't believe she made me come. I mean, I just got off the plane an hour ago."

I shrug, frowning. "Well, it's good you're here. I think Cassie could use the support."

"Well, she's not gonna get much from me. I'm just a kid."

I scrutinize Scout more closely. She's as old as me, but the look in her eyes makes her appear decades older. She stares at Cassie as the older woman chats up Lyle.

"I swear my aunt is starting to look like a candle. I mean, the side of her face looks like she's melting. Did you catch that foundation line?"

My eyes widen, as I let her words resonate.

She continues.

"I mean, for goodness' sake, the old crow couldn't do a paint by number."

I shoot Scout a harsh glare. "How long have you been here—like, two minutes?"

"Well, I'm getting a feeling about this place."

I could feel my blood pressure ticking up in my head. She hasn't been here long enough to get a "feeling" about Neelsville. "How's that?"

She smirks. "I can sniff out small-town bologna, and this place reeks of it."

You don't know the half of it.

I wanted to be offended, and yet there was something refreshing in her rudeness.

"You could be nicer, though—she did take you in."

Scout scoffs. "Yeah, well, I didn't want to be here in the first place. I really wanted to go to my other aunt's house. That bitch has got cash falling out of her slacks."

I cock my head. "Oh, really? Who might that be?"

"My Aunt Nilly. She lives on the West Coast, right off of Venice Beach. Cool as hell."

"Oh."

"And she's loaded! It didn't work out, though, so they bounced me over here."

She glances down at her sneakers and shrugs her shoulders.

"You move around a lot?"

"No. I'm just glad to be out of God damned Florida." She waves a dismissive hand in front of my face. "It's one hell of a place you know. And my mom's boyfriend can be a real prick."

My eyes narrow slightly. "How so?"

"Well, for starters, he likes punching holes in the walls, our walls are full of them."

"And, why would he do that?"

"Because he's one stupid son of a bitch, that's why. He places bets at the casino and then loses all his money. He's always giving them his paycheck. He does it every damn week, and he's too stupid to stop. So that's his name—that's why I call him, the prick.'"

"Oh, boy."

"'Oh, boy' is right."

Cassie hurries up to us.

"Scout, would you mind getting my sympathy card out of the car? I left it on the backseat."

Scout rolls her eyes, but she goes anyway after a quick "Alrighty."

I wait until she's out of hearing distance. "Wow."

Cassie leans in. "Don't I know it. Be careful with her—she's got a tongue like a razor."

"Is she here just for the funeral?"

"No. She'll be staying with us indefinitely, I'm afraid. She's getting to be too much for my sister—and apparently getting a little too friendly with some mayor down in Florida."

What?

"Really?"

"Yeah, and he's damn near my age, too. Old enough for an AARP card. Can you believe it?"

Cassie's one of those people that have no problem giving you all the dirty details with any topic, really. She is the most transparent person I know. After meeting a stranger, would have no qualms about discussing the timing of her bowel movements.

Cassie stares after where Scout had gone. "If she doesn't shape up, her next stop is boarding school."

I bite my lip, considering how Scout would fare at a boarding school. Probably not very well.

"I feel just awful for my sister; she doesn't know what to do anymore. With all the stunts Scout's pulled, I suggested she come here." Cassie's voice drops to a whisper. "And my sister, Linda, does not have the constitution to raise a girl like Scout! So, of course, she gets the wildest child in the universe. Isn't it funny how that works?"

"I guess. She did mention something to me, though."

"Oh, really? What's that?"

"Your sister's boyfriend? Apparently he likes punching walls. And um, gambling."

"Never heard of that."

Cassie stares down at her mud-splattered, half-broken heel before speaking.

"You know, sometimes you can do everything right, raise them the very best you know how, and they still manage to turn out all sideways."

Scout comes walking up then, card in hand, which she extends to her aunt. "Here ya go. Hope the food is good—I'm starving."

Cassie takes the card. "Alright, I best start mingling. I'll see you at dinner. And Scout, mind your manners, please. Try to make some friends your own age, know what I mean?"

"Yes, Aunt Cassie." Scout rolls her eyes again and leans in as her aunt heads away. "I think she has me confused with some six-year-old on their first day of school."

I try to hide my smile.

Scout catches my gaze, whispering, "If I see casseroles with crunchy toppings, I'm gonna shoot myself in the foot."

ART LIMEHOUSE

Art

"Hello, Dale?"

"Just one minute, sir." He could hear an annoying, rustling sound from the other end of the line. "Oh, yeah . . . Dale isn't here—he stepped out for an early lunch. Can I help you, sir?"

Art glances at his wristwatch and grimaces. It looked like someone smeared it with peanut butter. He's been meaning to get it replaced, but could never carve out the time. He noticed the band on it was getting frayed, and close to falling off his chubby wrist.

He squints to make out the tiny numbers through the smears, and a faint "10:30" comes into view.

Early lunch?

Art loathes being inconvenienced, especially by other people doing what he would much rather be doing, and that was eating. He lets out an exaggerated sigh, hoping the voice on the other end would catch his annoyance. He could start to feel his blood pressure ticking up, the heat of it tickling at the back of his neck.

"Well now, what kind of people start eating their lunch at 10:30 in the morning?"

He grins at his own comment. He can be a real asshole some-times—he can admit that, though not aloud, of course. In all honesty, people who ate lunch early were his kind of people, but they didn't have to know that.

He braces himself for the expected bile headed his way. He never subscribed to the notion of attracting more bees with honey.

"Well, sir, it's a working lunch. How can I help you?"

Oh, for heaven sakes.

"I'm **Dr. Limehouse,** Medical Examiner, ma'am—your office called me."

"Ohhhh, that's right, yes sir. Come to think of it, Dale has been wanting to speak with you."

Art huffs. "I know that, ma'am. Seems like we're playing a wild game of goose. Is there any way you can radio out that I called?"

Art could hear a heavy sigh from the other end of the line. "Sir, he's out in the *field.* It's unlikely he'll get any kind of a signal."

"Oh."

He pulls the phone away from his ear, stares at it for a second, and contemplates slamming it against the desk. He decides against it, for now.

The sing-songy voice rambles on as he puts the phone back to his ear. "I wish I could be of more help. He does call mid-afternoon for his messages; I can let him know you called."

"Please do so—it's of an urgent matter."

"Yes, sir."

He slams down the phone, leaving him unsatisfied and with a growling stomach—a double negative for Art. He's so hungry right now he could chew the knobs off his office door.

He glances over at the coffee station through his open door and spies a donut box.

Good Lord in heaven.

"Who brought in donuts?" he asks with a little more excitement than he wants to show. Like a toddler finding a lost toy, he couldn't get out of his chair and towards the coffee station quick enough.

Carlene's annoyed voice rings out as he approaches the station. "You know it's my birthday, right, Art?"

He stares down at the donut box, frowning. He didn't know that, but he doesn't really care, either. "Seems kind of backward, don't you think? I mean, it's your birthday—shouldn't you be the one getting the treat?"

She smiles sarcastically. "I don't make up the rules, Art."

Every year, Art needed reminding of this little tidbit of knowledge, because he could never seem to retain it. But he'll take any excuse for donuts.

His elation over donuts is short-lived, however, when he eyes the coffee pot. The carafe is bone dry, a dark ring of coffee is scalding the glass bottom, and smelling up the hallway. Art loathes the smell of burnt coffee, especially since Carlene's desk is close enough that she could have easily turned it off.

"Christ Almighty! Would it be too much to ask to keep the coffee pot full so we don't burn the damn place down?"

Art couldn't make a decent pot of coffee to save his life, but besides that, that's 'secretary work.'

Carlene narrows her eyes at him, but proceeds to make another pot anyway.

"Thank God for birthdays—and donuts," Art says as he spies a giant bear claw. Gotta love sugar, yeast, and flour. It was the simple things in life that made Art happy—and mad, for that matter.

He grabs another donut as Carlene finishes up the pot and heads back to her desk. Art pours himself another cupful, as soon as it's ready.

"Oh, and happy birthday, Carlene."

She doesn't look up from her typewriter, but her response is biting. "Thanks, Art."

He takes a sip of his coffee and finishes up the donut, pondering his next move as he saunters back to his office. He's found himself in a real mess here, and is unsure of his next steps.

He slumps to his desk chair, eyeing all the chaos that was on his desk. The paperwork alone was giving him hives the size of quarters.

His thoughts trail back to the state of his last patient. It will be weeks before toxicology will have any sort of reliable results, but he can't wait for that. He needs to get in touch with the authorities as soon as possible. If some random idiot is out there getting his rocks off by killing people with bow and arrows, then someone of authority needs to know about it.

Someone who knows what they are doing.

Art knew that when a person has a funny way dying, it tends to happen more than once. He didn't know what kind of clowns made up that department over there in Harvard County, but after what he just examined, he could feel the pit in his stomach grow larger by the minute.

He could count on one hand the few cases that had him mystified, and this is going to be one of them—he can feel it in his bones. He *knows* this is going to happen again.

He makes it his job to tend to every bit of his patients with the upmost care. Though he really shouldn't call them that—technically they aren't really his *patients*. They are already dead.

But he likes to think of them that way. He does everything in his power to try to figure out the last days or even hours of their lives, but sometimes his bosses didn't care for all that intensive meddling. It costs too much money and time. Being thorough has its share of drawbacks.

But he liked to think of it as a great service. Cherry picking through every possible detail of their deaths. And you would think that someone in the family would be more appreciative, but most never were.

But he can understand that. The grieving process has a way of twisting up a person's way of thinking, and clouding their judgement.

He isn't familiar with the townsfolk in Neelsville. But from what he's seen, he can't wrap his head around it. This bizarre murder—and he's quite certain that's what this is.

But it makes zero sense. The whole body looks like some charred piece of kindling found in some campfire horror flick. And to say the manner of death is fishy is, well, the biggest understatement put out into the universe.

He wipes the donut crumbs off his mustache, thinking back to the wound in the chest area of his last "patient." That was the fatal blow, the puncture area to the chest, and from the looks of it, it was made by a bow and arrow. But that still doesn't explain the strange markings and contusions visible on the forehead.

The rest of the body was burned beyond recognition, like a piece of toast. He turns it over in his mind, but he can't reconcile it, and the inconsistencies won't leave him alone. Usually, the answers could be found in logical explanations, most things could be. But not this time. This case is going to bug the hell out of him.

Art pushes to his feet and ambles back out to the coffee station where he pours himself a fresh cup, and grabs another donut. Two isn't going to cut it today.

So much for the diet.

He shrugs, scarfing down the donut before he makes it back to his desk and flops into his chair with a loud sigh. For now, he will need to set these worries aside so he can get on with his day.

He only hopes that Dale will return his call quickly.

BROOKE'S CHECKUP

Brooke

A storm is brewing, and the air feels heavy with rain. Right now, it's pounding so hard I wonder if the roof will cave in on top of us. I lift worried eyes up toward the ceiling.

An old man in the corner of the waiting room looks up from his paper, announcing the obvious. "Looks like it's raining cats and dogs out there."

Old people and their weather—they sure seem interested in it.

Despite the rain and everything that has happened, I'm still obligated to get my monthly allergy shot at Neelsville's only med center in the area, a clinic so old it's practically a relic.

The old man reeks of cigar smoke, but the stronger, stinging smell of alcohol is winning over. I notice it seems to be filtering in from the room down the hall. Odd, since this place looks about as sterile as a gas station bathroom.

For now, the allusion that life is back to normal has to be maintained. But considering everything I know about this town and what it's capable of, an allergy shot seems rather pointless.

Funny how the inner workings of denial can pollute the mind. It's such a powerful thing. That's probably how the distractors did it, but on a larger scale. And now I feel like I'm in on their little lie.

I glance over at Mom and Patti sitting beside me. She's been chewing the same wad of gum now for the past hour. I watch as she flips through a worn copy of whatever magazine she found on the table beside her, with so little interest she may as well be reading a math textbook.

I want so badly to tell Patti what's going on, but I didn't dare. I don't want to put her in any danger, so I continue to say nothing. Mom, too. *They can't know.*

Mom is busy transcribing her all-important grocery list. Much of her time is usually occupied by food, whether it be in the making or the planning.

This is the same clinic I went to when I was a little girl for my well-child checkups and monthly allergy shots. I never liked having to wait the twenty minutes afterward—there is never anything to do but just stare out the window. The other option is eye-balling the tiny lollipops in the chipped candy bowl. Just think, a sharp pin prick for a stale lollipop.

The lady at the front desk slides open the glass window. "Next?"

I jump to my feet and head over to the window. I notice the sliding glass is coated in fingerprints. I can't imagine looking through that thing all day and not cleaning it.

I nod once when I catch her eye. "I'm here for my shots."

"Name?"

"Brooke Larken."

"You need to have a seat. I will call you when we're ready."

No kidding. "Yes ma'am."

I watch as she closes the glass, and I get a glimpse of her long, catlike nails. She shoots me a displeased look as I search the waiting room for an empty chair. Mom and Patti didn't save me one, but I find another as far from Mr. Stale Cigar as I possibly can.

I hate dealing with crabby gatekeepers, it has a way of sucking the joy out of the day. It makes me wonder where Dr. Quincy is getting his help. You'd think he could find someone that didn't look like they spent all day sucking lemons.

Oh, that's right—the talk around town is that she was his cousin in need of a job. Well, that explains it.

I frown at the thought and turn to the magazine table, hoping to find one that isn't five years old.

There's an incessant tapping from the girl sitting across from me. She's been banging her foot into the chair next to her since I've been here. I want to tell her to stop, but she probably doesn't want to be here, either. I wish I could see her face—but it's buried in a yellowed copy of Reader's Digest. But there's something about the way she's sitting . . . her shoes even look familiar. And then it hits me: Is that Tammy? *The same Tammy who swapped spit with Dale Berkheist?*

I've been wanting to connect with someone from my class for the longest time, but the opportunity hadn't presented itself this entire summer. I can't seem to stop myself from saying her name out loud. "Tammy?"

She looks up from the magazine.

I wish, for the millionth time, that I could still read minds, but that ability has long left me. Being able to sniff out distractors without having to speak to them was such a wonderful gift—however short-lived—and not having it anymore felt cruel.

Her voice broke into my thoughts. "Hey, Brooke!"

I smile and ask a different question from the one I really wanted to ask.

Are you a monster yet?

"How have you been?"

There's an odd comfort in seeing an old classmate, even though we didn't really hang out together in high school. Even if she could potentially be a distractor. I try and chat with her a few more minutes. *Maybe I can tell.*

She rubs at her eyes, which look tired and swollen.

"You alright, Tammy?"

She sighs. "Yeah, it's just been hard to sleep lately. I'm here for my allergy shot, actually."

"Yeah, me, too."

"Hasn't it been crazy around here? I mean, with curfew and all that?"

I blink. "Curfew?"

"Didn't you hear?" She leans in a little. "There's been another murder, and they don't know who did it."

My back stiffens. "A murder? Where?"

"In Rhinetown."

Rhinetown was a small town about twenty minutes away. And this was not good news.

"It's probably a bunch of drug dealers, that's all," Mom chimes in from a few rows away, then continues with her grocery list.

"Well," Tammy starts, "after Ethel, they're not taking chances. This is such a loser of a town—I can't wait to leave here."

Tammy pulls at her tight, pink mini-skirt. In school she always dressed like she wanted action, and today is no different. I can't tell yet if she's a distractor, but I didn't think so.

I breathe out a sigh, my shoulders relaxing.

"The police are calling for a curfew—seems we're not safe outside after dark."

Patti, who'd interrupted her reading to eavesdrop on the conversation, turns her attention back to the magazine in her lap.

"It's only for two weeks," My mom says.

How could I not have known this?

Tammy nods. "The radio doesn't even broadcast anymore. There's nothing on TV except for static and, like, two channels."

"Tammy Zimmer," the nurse calls from the hallway.

I watch as she stands and walks toward the door, lost in my own thoughts. I really haven't been paying much attention to what's going on in the outside world, which includes avoiding the TV, radio, or any kind of news. But I had so many questions swirling around in my head, I wish her name hadn't been called so soon.

She turns around and winks before she slips through the door. "Wish me luck."

She steps out of sight into the small enclave. They're checking her vitals, and I can clearly hear everything the nurse is doing. I listen to her instructions as she puts on the blood pressure cuff on Tammy, her voice as loud as if she were attaching it to my own arm.

The walls around here must be made of particle board.

"Oh, dear," I hear the nurse say, "that's not right."

I snap my head in their direction, trying to hone-in on the conversation.

"Maybe it's broken," Tammy's voice offers.

A pause. "Well, that doesn't usually happen. Let's try again. I'm so sorry, dear."

I can hear the nurse pumping up the cuff again.

"Hmm, this is *strange.*"

Tammy speaks up. "That's okay—I have to be going now anyway. I can skip a shot."

"Are you sure, dear?"

"I'm sure, ma'am."

Before the nurse can say anything more, Tammy breezes on past us, opens the door, and walks herself out into the pouring rain. I run up to the window, trying to spot her in the parking lot, but she's already gone.

Well, that was weird. And why is she acting so strange?

"Brooke?" The nurse calls me back.

I stand and move robotically toward the door. Did I make a mistake? Is Tammy one of them, and I couldn't tell? Good Lord. I used to have good intuition—is that all gone now, too? I'm so screwed if I can't figure that out anymore.

The nurse sits me down right where Tammy had sat just minutes ago, her seat still warm.

And I can't help but ask. "So, the girl before of me—did she have a weird reading or something?"

The nurse furrows her brow. "Not at all. Why do you ask?"

"Oh, well, I just thought . . ." I stop right there. What's going on? Either she has short term memory loss or . . . Tammy did something to her so she wouldn't remember.

And Tammy isn't Tammy anymore.

Maybe I'm being paranoid. But the nurse did deny something that clearly just happened.

She leads me back to a room and gives me my shot. But before she can even put on the bandage, another nurse pokes her head in from the hallway.

"As long as you're here, the doctor would like to see you now."

I stare at her. "Me? For what?"

I don't remember having an appointment with the doctor. I was only supposed to be here for the shot.

"Oh, he wants to get to know his all patients, and he has a few minutes free right now, that's ok, isn't it?"

I guess so.

"Sure."

It's not like mom and Patti had anything significant to do, they could wait a few more minutes.

I follow the nurse down the hall to another room.

"He'll be in shortly," she says.

She closes the door, and I'm alone with my thoughts.

Good God, is it happening already? Is half the town full of these things? I sigh aloud.

Aaron, and Marcus, where the hell are you?

It was weird that the nurse blanked out when I asked her what went wrong and even stranger that Tammy just got up and left without getting her shot in the middle of a rainstorm.

And it's strange that I'm in this room. And how is it that this doctor has extra time? Don't they usually just stroll in after you've been waiting for a half hour, staring at the ceiling?

I don't know what to think anymore, as I scan the room, looking for anything normal. There's a colorful picture of the ocean framed in cheap brass hung on the ceiling, and there's a few rather prosaic, medical posters on the wall. Well, that's a start.

I shift on the crinkly paper covering the exam table, settling in. If he *is* the same doctor I saw at the funeral, maybe it would be good to meet him.

But I can't shake the feeling that he might be a distractor. I scan the room again, looking this time for something I can use as a weapon. Maybe a pair of scissors? I quick glance at the closed door, jump off the table and pull open the nearest drawer, scouting for anything that might work. All I see are vials of random medicine. Nothing major here.

I sigh. *This is ridiculous.*

Sure, these things are making their way here, but that doesn't mean the whole town is infected.

At least, not yet.

A tall man in white suddenly walks in, catching me in the act of snooping in his drawers. I jump, slamming the drawer closed without thinking about it.

"Hello, there! Looking for anything in particular?"

My face flushes, and I sink to a nearby chair. I think I catch a little smirk from him, but I'm not sure.

I feel the immediate need to apologize.

"Um, I'm so sorry."

My face couldn't get any more red—God, I hated that.

"I'm Dr. Cooper." He extends his hand, and I shake it.

"It's nice to meet you." He says, and I become aware that he is quite attractive.

I feel the need to explain myself.

"Sometimes I do that, sorry. Kind of a bad habit."

"What, opening drawers? Have you always been this curious?"

Good grief. Is he mad, or just playing with me? I didn't know him well enough to tell the difference.

He leans against the edge of the counter, a funny grin on his face. He didn't appear to be mad. But I don't answer his question.

"If you want, I can ask our secretary to show you our inventory list."

Yeah, she wouldn't be too keen on that, trust me.

"I'm good, thanks."

I want out of this room, but he steps toward me and extends his hand again, and with it comes the smell of his cologne. I don't know what kind it is, but it's far better than the smell of that stale waiting room. He doesn't appear to be mad—in fact, I see a tiny smirk playing at his lips at our touch.

He pulls away a second too late and leans back against the counter. "How are you today?"

"Other than curious? Pretty good, I guess."

My lame attempt at humor still quirks his lips.

It's nice of him to play things so cool, so I take a second to appraise him. He's taller than most of the people in Neelsville, with greenish eyes and a trim beard. He *is* rather attractive, but he's a doctor, which means, *stratospheric ego.*

"You're probably wondering why I called you back here."

"Ah, sure."

Still up against the counter, he casually flips through my chart, and smiles.

"Well, I just wanted to make sure you weren't suffering from some strange, exotic illness. And it's a good excuse to start getting to know some of my patients here in Neelsville. Dr. Quincy is seeing less patients these days, and I'm sort of the new guy in town."

"Yeah, I remember you. You were at the funeral."

What a dumb thing to say—he'd seen me there as well.

"Yes, rather unfortunate circumstances there. My condolences. I know Ethel was well thought of in this town."

He flashes me a full-on smile, and I avert my eyes. "Well, it was nice of you to attend."

He doesn't respond right away, his gaze penetrating. I'd hoped he would keep the conversation moving, since I didn't seem capable of it, but he just stares for a few moments. I think it should weird me out, but oddly, it doesn't.

He runs his hand through his hair and sighs. "A few of my patients here in Neelsville have been experiencing some, I don't know, rather unusual reactions, you could say."

Uh-oh. "What do you mean—reactions from shots?"

"No, this isn't from any kind of shot. More like random, flu-like symptoms."

I draw in a sharp breath and keep my voice steady. "Oh? What symptoms?"

"Well, like I said, it's unusual. The one thing they have in common is they have all lost feeling in one of their limbs. Sometimes two. We've already admitted several people to the hospital because of it."

People are in the hospital because they can't feel their arms? "Huh. That is weird."

"Yes. If there's a new strain of the flu, we'd like to get a handle on it. At this point, we're not quite sure what it is. But I do want to consider it carefully, proceed with caution."

"I haven't really noticed anything strange, not with me anyway." *Probably one of the biggest lies I've ever told.*

"Well, that's good news, then." He smiles again, which makes me fidget in my seat.

"So, no nausea?"

"Um, no."

"Then it's safe to say no loss of sensation in your limbs, either?"

"Not so far."

He nods. "Well, it would appear that you do not have any exotic virus."

"Good to know!" I grin, hoping my sparkling personality will get me out of this conversation A.S.A.P. *Get me out of this room.*

"Well, I'm glad to hear you're healthy. Hopefully, I won't have to see you again."

I frown at his comment.

"Oh, I didn't mean it that way. Of course, I'd like to see you again, just not under these circumstances. I'm sure I'll see you out and about in town."

I clear my throat as he pulls away from the counter and steps toward the door. "Yeah, I know what you meant. Um, have a good day."

He opens the door, and offers a final smile. "You too, Brooke."

As he walks out, I wonder if serendipitous and weird had ever mingled, that conversation would have been apart of it.

A part of me—a large part, if I'm being honest—is glad I made a connection with someone that isn't an alien or a crazy person. It feels nice to know that good, kind people are coming to our town. It gives me some hope that maybe we have a fighting chance.

But I still couldn't feel more alone if I tried.

Aaron is a distant memory. And I'm coming to terms with the possibility that I might never see him again. I try not to let myself go there.

I really don't know if I'll ever see him again, or any of his family, for that matter. I don't know how to protect myself or *my* family. And all I have are these fragments of info here and there of what's coming and what they're capable of.

I can feel it. Something big is coming.

AN AWAKENING

And I don't know how to stop it.

THE COUNTRY SINGER

Kaleb

It's a packed house at River's Edge Bar tonight. The owner, Margie, is doing her own bartending, and you gotta admire that. She's wearing some god-awful purple looking thing. But hell, she could wear a gunnysack and I would love her to pieces. She's one of the sweetest ladies I know. I hope she's heavy handed with the liquor, because I'm not much in the playing mood.

Some loud-mouth barfly is sitting up at the bar. I've been hearing her off and on for the past hour, and she's about as subtle as an elephant. She has one of those booming voices that demand to be heard. She's been crunching on the ice in her drink for the past half hour, and she has the most enormous dentures I've ever seen. I watch as she starts hitting on the guy to her left, then the right. She's the notable has been, *the flower that has already peaked.*

She passes her time here with loads of whimsy and flirtation. Intent on garnering full attention, and winning over all the males in the place. But for whatever the reason, she makes things interesting.

I watch as someone tells her a joke. She leans so far back into her stool that she about falls over. She laughs then, her voice rippling through the bar like a sour note. Her whole persona screams trouble, but the kind that might be fun in the sack. Or would have been—she's too old for me now.

Good God, I must be getting lonely.

Right now, to be honest, I don't want to talk with anyone. I just need to get through my next couple of sets so I can go home. Usually I'm not this fatigued at this point in the evening.

Better stick with water tonight.

The bar life has been my scene now for quite a while. In fact, it's so old, I could practically write the entire script. But lately, it's starting to feel like a bad movie on repeat.

People are, for the most part, warm and friendly. I can see it in their eyes, the excitement and admiration. But I don't know why they like me anymore, because I sure don't. Sometimes, when I get all this attention, I can't help but start to resent it.

All I ever wanted to do was write my own songs, play the guitar, and make enough to keep a roof over my head. If that resonates with people, well, that suits me just fine. And if it doesn't, that's okay, too, because I don't give a shit either way.

After my last set last week, some random woman came running up and tried cramming her tongue down my throat, but I shoved her away as politely as I could. They can get bold sometimes, and I just have to shrug it off. Just an overzealous fan that had too much to drink. Years ago, I would have been flattered, but now, not so much.

Over the years, I've been careful not to let many females into my life. Whenever I do, they have a way of causing me problems, and I don't need that in my life anymore. The truth is, I gave my heart to one long ago, and in return, she tossed it aside like a plastic, store grocery bag.

Thinking back on it, she had that irritating way of making me uncomfortable in my own skin. Probably one of the worst things a person can endure. And honestly, I had felt that way most of the time that we were together.

I find that it's easier now to keep things at a more surface level. I'm not looking to get into any new relationships, romantic or otherwise. If someone happens to catch my eye, I remind myself that a relationship just isn't in the cards for me. I've gotten quite good at this over the years, one might surmise that I've developed a callus around my heart. Well, so be it. Beats having it split open.

But even I admit, that at times, I feel like I'm a robot.

Every once in a while, I get little hints of hesitation, uncertainty, like maybe I need more of my own convincing.

Maybe I should take a chance on someone.

Then I have to remind myself of the promise I had made, that what's done is done, and I slam the door on these thoughts, before they spin out of control.

Reminiscing about lost loves doesn't get you anywhere but sad. Hell, because of it, I now have boatloads of content for some good old country songs. That's what it's all about, isn't it?

And yet . . . I can't shake the feeling that something is missing in my life. I'm doing everything right, I'm living my dream.

Why am I not happy?

Every few years, I take inventory on why I've become a singer in the first place, ask myself why I'm still doing this. It's silly really, I damn well know why. Making things right by a song is one of my favorite things to do, in all of this earth. It's righting all the wrongs in the world, wiping away its disease. Sometimes my emotions can spring up out of nowhere and get the best of me, which only makes me belt out the lyrics even louder.

There's a sort of magic that happens when I'm on the stage. I can feel the energy from the crowd, and it's a beautiful, innate connection between the two of us. One of the best feelings in the whole world.

Music expresses feelings that we can't say. It tells us that despite everything, things will work out the way they are supposed to, and that we're all on this adventure together.

When I'm on the stage, *I am my truest self.*

There are no rules, and I am free.

But the high of being on stage never lasts as long as I want it to. In fact, it's already slipping away as I'm packing up my equipment to go home.

And that used to be enough.

Sometimes I wonder how things would be if I had a regular job, got married, and had kids. I missed the boat on that one. But would that have been any better?

I think back to all the women that have drifted in and out of my life. Sure, they were fun. I can't help but smile at the giddiness of some of those women. Easy as the day was long, all smiley and dizzy just to get in a few words with me. And believe me, I thrived on that. I could chase that emotional buzz and make it last all week long. In my younger days, girls came and went like a revolving door, and believe me, I've had all kinds.

But that kind of life now is wearing on me.

Something's hitting me differently in the bar today. I don't know what it is, but I can *feel* it.

There's an elevation to the room that hasn't been here before, a kind of vibration. That's the best way I know to describe it.

I had noticed it towards the end of my last set. I was on my final song, the one I've sung a hundred times before, and my heart had picked up a beat. Like it was responding to something I didn't know, and I didn't understand it. I know it sounds crazy, but it was just a general feeling of unease.

It feels like I'm getting ready to jump off a cliff.

I do a quick scan of the room as I finish up my current set. There doesn't appear to be anything unusual. The regular drunks in the front are slurring their words, laughing out loud, and washing it all down with PBR. People are starting to crowd the stage.

Sometimes women like to dance a few feet away from where I sing, flaunting themselves like drunken peacocks, gyrating their hips this way and that. Like that's supposed to turn me on. I admit, sometimes it does—I am male after all—but other times . . .

There's a woman like that right now, dancing a few feet away from me, and way too close to my mic stand. Every few seconds, her hand swings up and smacks it as she dances, causing it to rock back and forth in its place. I know in her boozy state she could care less about boundaries, but I'm well aware. I ignore it the first couple of times it happens, but after each time, I can feel myself getting angrier.

It's just a mic stand.

I can't tell you all the times aimless drunks have crashed into me, sending my equipment flying all over the place and me sprawling to the floor. Drunks don't care what they do.

A strange pygmy of a man is facing the dancing fool, and from the admiration in his eyes, I guess he's the significant other. He has that glazed-over, dipshit look only alcohol can accomplish, and his eyes are transfixed on her dancing. He's watching her butt, and his smirk says, *"I'm getting lucky later!"*

What do I know? He probably is. My guess is he's supposed to be making sure she doesn't fall or break an ankle right there on the dance floor. *And he is severely lacking in his responsibilities.* And they are eyesores, the two of them.

There will always be women like her clinging to the stage, wearing jeans so tight someone would think they were spray-painted on, the smell of hairspray, sweat, and cheap beer swirling about the bar like some hedonistic perfume. God, I both love and hate this scene.

By the end of my second-to-last song, the annoying dancer finally leaves the floor and makes a beeline for the bathroom.

Praise Jesus.

For the first time that evening, I feel like I can take in a solid breath. I finish the last of my set, and glad for the break. If I don't make my way to the bathroom, there will be a mess on the floor.

When I finish, I saunter into the main room and up to the bar.

God, I need a drink. And water isn't gonna cut it.

The barfly notices me, and I try ignoring her, but she's sitting mere feet from the bartender. She glances over and asks me a question. "What's your dime, partner?"

"Excuse me?"

"Drink, son. What's your drink?"

One great perk of being a singer—the drinks are always free. "Jack and Coke."

Margie walks over and pours a generous amount into the shot glass and slides it over.

I'm not in the best of moods, and I could use some mellowing out. And if Jack can't do the job, nothing will. I need something extra to get through this next set.

And it never used to be this way.

I watch as a girl walks up to the bar, directing a question at Margie.

"Where's all the cherries?"

"Over there, girlie, and please don't pick them out with your fingers—it's gross."

She leans over the bar, and I watch as she sneaks a handful anyway, while Margie tends to another customer. I find her manner peculiar, and clearly cavalier with the rules. It's both intriguing—and refreshing.

She looks in my direction.

"What are you looking at?," she says.

I can't help but smile. I'm so surprised by her demeanor that I don't know how to answer her, not properly anyway. I just stare.

She nods at my Jack and Coke. "Maybe you should tend to your drink."

She doesn't seem to have any sort of filter.

A voice comes from my other side. "Last set wear you out, honey?"

It's the barfly. I swear to God, if I have to make small talk with her before I finish my drink, I'll want to shoot myself in the head.

She takes a long drag of her cigarette, blowing it out towards the ceiling. "Have you played here long?"

"Years."

She smiles and continues. "Ya know, one of these days you're gonna hit it real big. And then, wham-bam, stardom. You know that, right?"

Funny she would mention that. After the encounter I had the evening before, I *did* know it. She interrupts my thoughts.

"I'm like a bloodhound with these things. And you know what?"

I turn toward her. "What's that?"

"I can smell it on you."

I can't help but grin. Drunks can be as charming as they are ridiculous. But she is right about one thing—according to the documents I signed less than twenty-four hours ago, fame will finally find its way to me.

Finally.

I don't know what to expect, but I'm ready to experience it. Heck, I was ready twenty years ago.

Margie looks up from her bar, a scowl on her face. "Leave him alone, Cassie. Can't you see he's trying to talk to Brooke? You're not in the game anymore, darling."

Saved by the bartender.

"I'm just admiring his obvious sparkle is all," Cassie shoots back.

"Oh, *gawd.*" Margie rolls her eyes.

"I'm sorry, Kaleb—she's not usually like that."

"You're a liar, Margie; I'm very much like that. I just like living life emphatically. What's wrong with that? By the way, I'm getting dry over here—could you snap to it with the drinks?"

"Like a hole in your head," Margie mutters, but she makes another drink for her anyway.

The girl with the cherries chuckles, drawing my attention back to her. She's tall, statuesque, and I bet intimidates the hell out of the guys around here.

And I can't shake the feeling that I've met her once before.

I pinch my eyebrows together, squinting at her as subtly as I can. Yes, I'm quite certain that I know her, but for the life of me, I can't place where we've met.

I nod, hopefully before she thinks I'm weird for staring.

"I'm Kaleb."

Her mouth turns up in the faintest of smiles. "Nice to meet you."

She stares at me. I wait for her to say her name, but she doesn't.

I try again. "Have I met you before?"

There's that subtle feeling of unease, paying me a little visit, and I do my best to shake it off.

What is going on?

She frowns. "I don't think so."

I notice her eyes have a rather illuminating quality, and in the remarkable shade of electric blue. It's the kind that's hard to look away from, and I feel a bit trapped in her gaze.

I scan my brain for where I could have possibly met her. Another bar perhaps? No, she's a little young for that. At a Summerfest concert? Maybe, but surely I would have remembered her...

Out of the corner of my eye, I see a drunk at the back of the bar. He's got that drunk, dodgy eyed stare. I notice he's been watching her every move. I don't care for him looking at her, and I'm surprised at how quickly my anger surfaces. *God, he better not come over here.*

Unfortunately, that's exactly what he does. Well, drunks and good sense have never gone together anyway. I eye him carefully, bracing myself for trouble, knowing it's coming.

He stands there, about a foot away, and scans her up and down. She pretends not to notice, but I sure do.

"God damnit, you're tall."

Her face flushes, but manages a smile. "No kidding."

"You gotta be about six feet, huh?"

I notice the slight twang in his words. He isn't from around here. His clothes look fancy, and his cologne smells expensive. I can see white drool attached to the corner of his lip like an ornament, and I'm repulsed. I loathe dealing with these kinds of drunks—and the rich ones are the worst.

I come to the young woman's defense before things get out of hand. "Get the hell out of here."

"You gonna make me?"

I jump to my feet, feeling fire run through me as I confront him. I'm shocked at how ready I am for a good bar fight—it's been way too long.

I want him to throw the first punch so bad, please, *give me a reason*. Any excuse to beat him to a bloody pulp.

Let me feel something. Though I wonder, if it ever gets to that point, would I be able to stop?

Margie steps in. "Leave right now, mister, or I'm calling the cops! Be smart, and walk yourself out the door."

The drunk, realizing he's outnumbered, finds his way towards the door, but not without getting a few choice words in. "Lame ass bar, if you ask me." "We didn't!" Margie calls after him just before the door slams shut.

I glance over at the tall girl with the electric eyes. Her cheeks are red, her eyes hidden from my view. "Sorry about that."

She attempts a smile, and it warms my insides. "It's okay. It's a curse."

"What is?"

"Being tall. I hate it."

I shake my head. "Don't, it suits you."

"Well, none of the guys around here seem to think so. They hate tall girls." She frowns and turns toward our bartender. "Almost ready, Margie?"

"Sure, hon." Margie wipes a rag over the counter in front of her and nods toward the door. "That jerk won't be allowed here anymore."

She nods at Margie's declaration, but I'm stuck on her question, so I decide to ask. "Did you order some food?"

She crunches up her nose. "No. I'm here for my dad actually; grocery order." She manages a smile, but it doesn't reach her eyes.

Margie hands her a brown bag. I can see the telltale bottle of Kessler Whiskey and a carton of smokes inside. "Tell Rich I said hello."

"Sure, Margie."

My eyes follow her as she heads toward the door, she lingers for a bit, and looks my way.

"Hey, thanks for that."

"Oh, sure."

As she walks away, it hits me.

She never told me her name.

I want to know who she is, it's now or never. *You're breaking your own rules,* a voice warns in my head, but I don't care. In a few seconds, she'll be gone, and I want to know her name. I *need* to.

I'm not sure if I will ever see her again, so I make an impulsive decision and follow her out the door.

"Hey, you never told me your name."

She spins around. "It's Brooke."

I smile. I've always liked that name.

As she turns and walks away, I feel it again, that tugging, uneasy-yet-not-unpleasant sensation rising up in my chest.

There's no denying it now. However crazy this sounds, I feel like a small part of my life has just walked out that door.

THE CONTRACT

~*The Night Before*~
Kaleb

*A*fter a quiet dinner alone, I step outside for a walk, not unusual for me, I love this time of year. There's nothing I enjoy more than a quiet walk through the woods. It's the only way I can relax, and decompress.

I much prefer the solitude and clean air of the outdoors to surface-level conversations anyway. Charlie is with me; we're full-time buddies now. I picked him up a few weeks ago from the dog rescue, and I tell ya, it's been one of the best decisions I've ever made in my life. He's been my constant companion ever since.

When I first saw him there last month, I knew I had to have him. It feels pretty good knowing I got him out of there, and now he can live out the rest of his life with me. We rescued each other, really. Charlie has taken the sting out of living alone, and there isn't much else I need more than him.

I notice early on in our walk that Charlie seems a bit unsettled. He keeps staring ahead of us into the woods, with a continuous, low growl. He's detecting something I haven't seen yet.

"What's up, boy?"

I give him a pat hoping to reassure him, but he continues to growl at the darkened woods. I bend down, crouching beside him, and follow his gaze.

And that's when I notice it: Things *do* feel different today. I hear a constant barrage of caws from several different birds overhead, and Charlie stops his growling long enough to yelp out a few harsh barks.

I narrow my eyes, squinting into the woods, and they shoot wide. I leap to my feet, stumbling backward. Someone is in the woods, standing amongst the trees.

Usually, I get a sense of someone before I see them. Not today, I guess.

"Can I help you sir?" I call out.

As he steps out of the woods and into the clearing, I notice his extreme height. He's wearing all black, the choice of color a bit menacing against the backdrop of the inky woods.

At first, he just stares at Charlie and me, ignoring my question. He isn't moving at all, which makes me take an instinctive step back.

As I do, he answers. "No, sir. But I can help you. I was wondering if you might be open to having a little chat? I know I'm trespassing here"—he's right; there are no-trespassing signs posted everywhere throughout these woods—"but I promise, it will be well worth your while."

I raise an eyebrow at his proposition. The last thing I want to do tonight is talk to a salesman.

The strange man moves in closer, his gait displaying a rather unusual cadence that looks unnatural and odd. Watching him walk is giving me goosebumps, and he seems to sense this.

"You'll have to excuse me; I'm rather awkward in these circumstances."

I hold in a snort.

Creepy is more like it.

"Let me introduce myself. I am, *Avalone*." He emphasizes the last syllable like he's announcing a distinguished title.

I blink at him. "I don't think I've ever heard of such a name."

"It is somewhat, unusual," he concedes. He laughs then, causing a stir amongst the nearby wildlife…I hear them scattering about in the woods. If I had to guess, I would say he is in some sort of hallucinogenic state.

"Let's just say I'm of the most supreme of beings, and leave it that, shall we?"

Did he just say he was "of the most supreme of beings"? Delusions of grandeur, much? "Look, sir, this is private property—I think you should be going."

"Oh, do you now? Aren't you at all curious about what I have to say?"

Not in the least, I want to say, but I stay quiet. It's way past time for him to go. And if he isn't going to, then I will.

As I turn, pulling on Charlie's leash, I feel an immediate sting at the back of my neck.

The ridiculous thought of *bees wouldn't be around at this hour* shoots through my mind as my hand touches the spot—and my skin feels hot to the touch.

"Please, formalities are such a chore; there's no need to leave. I think we got off on the wrong foot here."

I turn around slowly, staring as I rub my neck. My eyes scan down his formidable body, and it's then that I notice his nails.

Why are they so long? Their about as long as a grizzly bears.

He, of course, sees my reaction. "Oh, I've frightened you; I do apologize. We don't consider it appealing to shorten our nails, although it probably would make life around here easier. I'm sorry."

I stare at their astounding length, and wonder how he manages daily living.

He couldn't possibly. My unease grows.

Avalone extends his long hand, and I have to remind myself that this is just a handshake as his long nails drag across my palm. I drop his hand quickly, fighting the urge to wipe mine on the leg of my pants.

He speaks first. "Kind of a solitary place you have here."

I cross my arms. "That's the way I like it."

"Hmm, I understand."

This guy's bravado is getting under my skin. And I still don't know why he's here.

"I'm sorry, um, what did you want to chat about?"

He grins as he contemplates his next words.

"Let me start with this: energy transference."

"Excuse me?"

"Yes, I believe that's the correct term, and it's evident in this entire block of woods, I'm afraid."

Avalone exudes confidence with his dark demeanor, and I feel like I should know what he's talking about, but I don't have a clue.

"What is?"

"You, your energy."

"I'm sorry—*my energy?*"

"Yes. Think of it as a genetic footprint. I can see it just as clear as you can see other tangible things—like the ground we stand on, for instance."

"Come again? I don't know that I follow."

"You wouldn't, and I don't expect you to. But, for example, while you were making your chili last night, you were wondering what it would have been like to have a life partner."

I recalled maybe feeling a little bit like that, but it was a fleeting moment. And how the heck would he know that? *And how did he know I made chili?!*

"It's a rather pitiful state to be in, don't you think?"

My eyes narrow. "I hate to disappoint you, Avalone, but I don't feel sorry for myself at all. I think you should probably go." I'm more than done with this guy now.

"And throw away the chance you have to be more? Come on; you can't tell me you don't feel it. It's permeating this entire place, I'm afraid. And it's all over you. Not a good look, by the way."

My eyes widen. Part of me is terrified, but the other part is drawn to what he is saying.

I strengthen my stance. He knows things he can't possibly know, like what I was thinking last night and the chili thing. Which leads me to one conclusion: He's been spying on me.

"Listen, you should leave. Get off my property before I call the cops."

"Look, they can't help you. Not like I can. You're almost to the point where you're not teachable; however, I have been known to work miracles."

My head swims, I feel as if I've stumbled upon another realm, one where he is the creature in charge, dishing out ridiculous absolutes. And I don't know the rules of any of it.

If I was a pinball machine, right now it would be on full tilt.

"I can sense what's inside you, your emotions. They're swimming around in that exquisite brain of yours. It's too large for your own good, I'm afraid."

"What is that—my brain?"

Avalone laughed again, deeper this time. "Your ego, son. That thing needs a leash; it's a monster."

"*My ego?*"

"Yes! It's raging in you, and in such an unhealthy state. But no worries—I can teach you to use it properly, become a force to be reckoned with."

This guy can't be serious. I feel like I just bumped into a Johnny Cash wannabe in the middle of a coke binge.

"Think of it as a rocket ship on the way to space, my friend. However, instead of burdening yourself with all the loathsome particulars, everything will simply be taken care of."

"I'm sorry, what will be taken care of, exactly?"

"Only one of the greatest gifts bestowed on a human being—other than life itself, of course. I don't expect you to understand, but you will."

"Well, I'm doing just fine on my own."

"Are you now? Maybe things will work out for you just the way you planned. Or maybe you'll be in an accident next week and miss your chance at greatness. Keep doing things the way you've always done them, and that's what you'll get. A great big, fat, *maybe.*"

I didn't need a lecture on all the hard work needed to get into stadiums—I know what it takes. Lots of my blood, sweat, and tears go into every show, and along with that, a little bit of luck. It really was about timing. But truthfully, it hasn't gotten me to where I really wanted to go.

I've always wanted to be well-known, and here this terrifying being in black is offering it up to me like a piece of candy.

"Are you an agent?"

He smiles, an unsettling sight on his weathered face. "I'm a special kind of one. I fix troubled minds and polish them up like a pretty penny."

I scrub my hand over my face, wishing I hadn't gotten drunk last night. Because the longer I stand next to Avalone, the less spurious his intentions appear. I'm finding it difficult to discern the truth of what he's saying to me, the lines blurring the more he speaks. And that's a dangerous place to be, me, starting to believe him. However crazy he sounds.

"I happen to have an alternate philosophy when it comes to alcohol. It's just truth serum at its finest. Sometimes people just need to hear a good dose of the truth, don't you think? *In vino veritas.*"

He reveals a toothy grin then that makes me turn away.

"Unspoken words and thoughts, heartfelt confessions . . . Get some of the spirits in you, and there they all come, swimming up to the surface. Just waiting to spill out all over the pavement, like a crowd of long-lost pals at a beach party."

I don't utter a word, so he continues.

"Did you know that true empathy can only be felt if a person has had a particular trauma in their life?"

That felt true, but I didn't want to admit that to him.

"It is true, my friend! You can still feel sorry for them—on the surface, of course." He takes a breath. "That's the gift of adversity. People who experience it gain such great insight and knowledge. Consider it a peace offering from the universe. A prize for having to deal with a rather repugnant event they might have experienced. Sort of like when Eve took a bite of the apple—and when she did, she saw things as they truly were. There was no veil of comfort anymore."

He sighed. "Anyway, I'm getting off on a tangent here. Let's get down to the nuts and bolts of it, shall we? What I'm offering here is a one-time deal; and will not be offered again."

"And you're offering me *fame?*"

"Ding, ding, ding. Tell him what he's won, Wally."

I stand there, staring. Part of me feels punch drunk, my insides a jumbled mess of chaos. The other part--the sober part—feels hard to conjure up. It's void of thought--like I lost all my words and how to think for myself.

I wanted then just to retreat back to the safety of my warm house and forget any of this ever happened. But whatever musings that Avalone is spitting out, it *feels* true. However ridiculous and strange it may have sounded at the beginning, is now, starting to resonate.

Maybe I'm under some sort of spell, but this spell is starting to feel right.

"Creative people usually have one foot stuck in the dream world while the other dangles in reality. Such a precarious position to be in, but that's the nature of the beast, isn't it? You have to be a little crazy to reveal what is truly in your soul."

My teeth are chattering so loudly, I'm sure Avalone notices. And meanwhile, my warm house still awaits. I don't know how he can stand this cold—his clothing looks paper thin.

"I will leave it up to you," he says, as he produces a small stack of papers that looks like a contract. It's strange how they seem to appear out of nowhere; and I didn't recall him carrying anything. "You'll just need to look these over."

He didn't mention anything about a contract, either, and yet, here it is. I try not to notice the menacing features of Avalone, as he shows me the papers. The font on them looks fancy, and there is a gold seal at the bottom, giving it an air of legitimacy.

"Contract?"

"The most important one you'll ever sign."

I can't afford this.

"How much is this gonna set me back?"

Avalone threw his pointy head back, his boisterous laugh echoing throughout the dark woods. "Your money is no good here. Besides, it doesn't exist in our organization."

That's weird.

"What kind of organization doesn't deal with money?"

"Only the most important one in the universe. We are above such trivial matters. You need to start thinking of money as more of an energy exchange. And when you become a part of our team, you'll start to see these things more clearly."

I've never been a fan of contracts—looking at them always left my stomach in knots. The devil is in the details, so they say.

And that saying has never felt more true than it does tonight.

But a contract is necessary if one doesn't want to get screwed over, and I'm not in the habit of signing things I haven't read. My eyes scan the page, noting the fairly standard terms before landing on the name scrawled in red font at the bottom of the page.

Brooke Larken

"Who's this?" My eyebrow raises.

Avalone huffs. "Ah, yes. A rather unfortunate sort."

I continue listening, but my expression doesn't change.

"Allow me to elaborate. She is a rather unappealing in character, offensive in nature, into trickery and lies. Are you getting my drift?"

"Yeah, I'm thinking you don't like her."

He starts laughing. "Good guess, my friend. But I wouldn't waste your time with her, unless, of course, you would rather be *un*-famous."

I can't help but burst out laughing. I have always been *un*-famous.

"Suffice it to say, she's just the type to take you off your well-deserved path."

This guy must really hate her.

"Well, I don't know anyone named Brooke."

"Ah, but you will."

I shrug, frowning. "Okay."

"We have eyes everywhere."

I didn't doubt that. I'll have to watch my back and keep my nose clean if I sign this contract.

Because in this moment, as I'm standing here shivering in the cold, I realize that I *will* be signing this contract, and giving in to Avalone's demands. My head aches, and I long for an end to this worrisome conversation.

I pinch the bridge of my nose, squeezing my eyes shut until I hear his scratchy voice again.

"Do pay attention, please."

I open my eyes to meet his unnerving gaze and clear my throat. "Will do."

"Sign here, and I will get it notarized. A delivery man will bring it to you in the morning. Getting up early is not a problem for you, is it, singer?"

"No, it's not a problem."

Avalone gave a sinister grin. "That's great to hear."

I don't mind early appointments, but I can't seem to shake off my anxiousness. All I want is to sign these papers so he can go.

"When the contract is notarized and physically in your hands tomorrow morning, at that moment, it will be binding."

I can't believe I'm doing this, and yet, this feels like the change I've been looking for.

Avalone materializes a pen out of thin air. It's long and ornate, and feels fitting for what I'm about to do. A tug of hesitancy pulls at me, but I shrug it off and scratch my name at the bottom of the page. Snow starts to fall all around us, and Avalone's eyes light up as I sign the third and final page.

He repossesses the pen and paper, tucking them back into his long, black coat. Again, I notice the grizzly nails, and I can't help but shiver. "I'll be going now, but we'll be meeting soon."

As he saunters off toward a car--which I could've sworn wasn't there a minute ago—a shiny black Mustang, of all things—I catch another glimpse of those terrifying nails. They look even longer than I remember from earlier in our conversation, and sticking out of the sleeves of his dark coat like daggers. Can he look any more menacing?

And were they really that long just a minute ago?

As the sound of the car fades away, the eerie fog in my brain starts to lift. I blink over and over again, trying to come out of what feels like a trance. *What just happened here?*

I swallow hard, pushing away my suspicions that this may have been a half-baked idea. But that's okay—I'm a pro at internalizing things, and what's done is done.

I also ignore the fact that throughout our entire meeting, Charlie maintained a steady, even growl, something I hadn't even realized until this moment. Ever the protector, he never left my side.

MR. SARDINE

Mr. Sardine

*M*r. Sardine has a gut on him that extends way beyond the limits of what a belt is expected to do. But that is just his way, always stretching things out to full capacity.

He glances in the rearview, getting a better look at his pockmarked face and beady eyes. God, he loathed the way he looked. He always has. His only hope is when he becomes a full-blown distractor, he can finally do something about it.

Today's delivery is going to be an important one; and that's all he was told. The higher-ups never discuss any of the details where it involves the personal matters of their subjects. They just expect him to do his job, which is delivering contracts, and to never ask questions about the people involved. And he never does either, and that's why they like him.

He glances down at the address on the paper, it's written in sloppy cursive, but he can still make it out. It takes him awhile to find this house, there are no real landmarks—it's one of those out-of-the-way kind of places that's hard to find on a map unless, of course, you stumble upon it by accident. Finding this one though, takes a bit more detective work, but then again, Sardine isn't your ordinary deliveryman.

Often he likes making a game out of finding some of these house stops. Like trying to solve a puzzle. Houses without numbers, houses that look like little matchboxes that one would often pass by, thinking it's just a glorified shack. Not realizing that someone actually *lives* there. And Sardine is no stranger to finding places out in the middle of nowhere.

As soon as he drives up to this house, he hears the dog, and even after a few minutes of sitting in his van, the barking isn't letting up. He feels a heavy pounding in his head as he scans the house's exterior and turns off the ignition.

He hates having to deal with the pets of these flighty souls. The worst part of his job really, the pets always catch on far sooner than their owners—especially when it comes to the unseen.

The irony isn't lost on Sardine. Animals can long see the intuitive path much clearer than any human ever could. Humans are usually the last to figure it out, funny, because they're the ones signing the contracts.

Before he presses the doorbell, he senses the owner at the other side of the door. As it opens, he stands before him, a resolute look in his eye. Sardine is glad he's expected—it makes his job easier, and he can soon get on with his next delivery.

The incessant barking from the dog, however, is getting on his nerves. The dog knows what Sardine is becoming. *And he loathes being reminded of it.*

"Your paperwork, sir."

He makes a quick mental note—this homeowner is polite but disheveled, he can smell the man's foulness from the night before, it radiates from the pores on his skin. Being a near distractor himself, all his senses are heightened. But this man's appearance at the door is not atypical according to Sardine's log—he's much like all the others. He scans him with pity. The man's weariness isn't lost on him; Sardine knows the scenario all too well.

He stares at the person who all the higher-ups are having a field day over. He's a singer, but to Sardine, he's just another soul, another feather in the distractor's cap.

He answered the door with a coffee mug in hand and a twinkle in his eye, despite his fatigue. He notes that he is both mannerly and pleasant, which, considering the state of things, a darn shame.

Sardine eyes his coffee cup, thinking a nice cup of coffee would be perfect right about now.

The singer senses this. "Oh, would you like some coffee?"

Now we're talking. "I would love some, thanks."

He comes back with a fresh mug, the steam rising off the surface. Sardine almost wishes he wasn't so darn agreeable—he's bargaining with his fate, after all. But, alas, that's the way of it, sometimes.

Sardine takes a long sip. "Be sure to look these over. There's just one more to sign, and I'll be on my merry way."

"Ah, yes. Mr. Black said you'd be stopping by today."

Sardine knew there was something different about this particular contract. The color was slightly different, and the papers had a sturdier feel. His boss was adamant that they be signed—and Sardine hoped he didn't have any specific questions. But if he did, he wouldn't even know how to answer them. Fine print always made both his eyes twitch when he was still full human, even if he wasn't the one signing them. But the higher-ups assured him that all of the details had been taken care of the night before, and the singer should be well aware of everything he needed to know.

All that was needed, was a signature.

He notices Kaleb patting his t-shirt. "Never a pen when you need it."

"Not necessary, sir; I have one right here."

Sardine produces a pen in gunmetal grey. He can feel the singer's ghosts lingering around him, hanging about in the corners of his house. Loneliness, uncertainty, regret. He doesn't envy him his demons.

Once the singer is done signing the papers, Sardine knows first-hand what he will be feeling. For starters, all of the emptiness he is feeling will start to fall away. As the day wears on, the effects of becoming a distractor will start to take its hold. The aging process will begin to stop. There will be less of a need to use the bathroom. Eating will become more of a choice, rather than a need.

Funny thing is, Sardine often thought entertainers to be a funny lot. So much talent they can give the world, and yet, still all these damn problems.

Hell, he delivers packages for a living, and he is right as rain. Well, as right as one can be when you just signed away your soul.

Just goes to show that even with all the talent in the world, no amount of praise can close the dark hole looming in one's heart. Sure, it can soften the edges, but there would still be that hole.

"You'll need to put these in a safe, you know; they're important. Got one?"

"I do, actually."

Sardine hands him the papers with a clipboard so he can sign it. He's going through the motions here. There is no possible way of destroying these papers. They could be in the middle of a forest fire, and yet, they would still be sitting there amongst all the dead and charred wood. These kinds of documents are indestructible, and he delivers hundreds of them every year, all over the world.

"You want to come in?"

"No, thank you, sir. I've got a boatload of deliveries, but I appreciate the coffee." He smiles, and Kaleb smiles back.

The reactions of humans always made him take pause, reminding him of what he is or will soon become. Sometimes, it's a hard thing to witness. Maybe it's the human part of him still rejecting the distractor traits, one last fight before taking the plunge, as it were.

He'll be glad when all his human feelings will just go away.

It just makes things easier.

Signed papers in hand, Sardine walks back down the sidewalk, tempering his urge to kill the dog. He can not give in to his urges, especially now. Going down a last-minute rabbit hole would be a stupid thing for him to do. He's still proving himself, and darn close to his delivery goal. Petty annoyances cannot get the best of him.

Sardine plops back into the driver's seat of his van, the shocks complaining as he does, and congratulates himself on yet another successful delivery.

He pulls out his journal, placing a checkmark next to this address.

Successful delivery!

He isn't full distractor yet, but soon will be—he has roughly 250 more deliveries before he becomes one. And he makes note of it in his journal. This journal of his, is the most important thing he has ever written.

As he pulls away and heads out to his next stop, he lets everything sink in. He still can't believe they chose him of all people, and they let him in on their dark secret. And oh, the things he was promised! One of them being his promotion to CEO of UFS deliveries. This is where he will be in charge. And he'll finally be able to run an organization however he sees fit.

And he had never been in charge of anything in his life!

Sardine slams on the brakes, letting a deer pass across the road. As he waits, he glances back at the large stack of papers resting on the seat behind him.

Wow, they are still sizzling!

He notices the three contracts, they are in the passenger seat beside him, in a full blaze of fire. He has two more of these to deliver today, all in a hundred-mile radius.

They are on fire because they are newly minted. The edges of the papers make these little crackling noises, making him think he's sitting next to a fire. He tries to ignore the pieces of blackish confetti swirling about inside the van. The upholstery is already covered in soot. He tries wiping it off the dash, but that does very little. The van had been detailed only last week, but considering his line of work, it's impossible to maintain.

These souls must be extra special—*contracts don't burn this bright and for so long.*

Bits of charred paper continue to fall, some of it shiny, as it catches the light. It's all around him now, making the inside of his car look like the end of a New Year's Eve party. Except, this one was for dead, lost souls.

He eyes the singer's contract, and looks at his watch. It's been a good twenty minutes now since it's been signed, and it's still on fire. The other contracts have died down, but not this one.

He knows most contracts are only on fire for a few minutes at a time, but the special ones, the ones that are of particular interest to the distractors, are always on fire the longest.

CHASING GHOSTS

The Traveller

I do not want to come back to this town, and God knows I have a thousand reasons why. However, my wife Penny insists.

The things we do for the people we love.

Things became strange as soon as we cross into the state of Illinois. We have to stop for gas, a rather droll activity I particularly loathe, but I hate it even more when Penny has to do it.

I know things are peculiar here as soon as I step out of the car. For starters, I'm alarmed by the state of the woods across the street. There's a sort of vapor clinging amongst the trees and there's strange sounds in the air, too. They sound like simple birds for all intents and purposes, but I know better.

The woods are full of these things; in fact, I am certain that one is watching me now. I cross to the side of the car that holds the gas tank and place the pump in the tank as I take full inventory of the three souls nearest to me. This is an old habit of mine—I don't care to be caught off guard. But these souls are just, well, tired. I can tell they don't like pumping gas, either; they just want to top off the tank and get back on the road. And all are very much human.

This is the precise reason I don't care to go anywhere. I'm like a sponge, soaking up all the anxious and uneasy thoughts of those around me, which—by the way—take forever to expel. I can overthink things to the point of ad nauseaum, and I only make it worse because I have vast amounts of time to do it.

So, in essence, I am my own problem.

I can now smell distractor in the area. Their aroma is so repulsive to me, I can barely fight the urge not to puke. I glance around and see someone getting out of a rundown van, presumably to pump gas. *There you are.* I'd hoped I would have gotten used to the smell by now, but it hits me hard every time. And though he just arrived, I know he is the one radiating this revolting smell.

I'm so not in the mood for this.

The evil within him is so clear in my mind, I'm astounded that the humans around me cannot detect it. But that's okay—I know their abilities are not as far-reaching as mine.

As a rule, I don't care to intervene in the lives of humans, but after reading a good portion of his mind, I realize that he needs to be expelled from this earth, and the sooner the better. I'll consider it a "cleaning up" of sorts.

His thoughts tell me of a monstrous evil he's planning for the family getting gas right in front of him, and I want no responsibility for that calamity.

The old me would have walked away, but not this time.

I wait until he gets back in his car, and when no one is looking, I pull out my trusty dagger. I usually have it nearby, especially on road trips; I'm always prepared for the unexpected. With furtive glances side to side, I approach the vehicle, climbing into the back seat before he has a chance to put the key into the ignition.

And then, I gut him right there like a fish. Just a quick slice across his throat.

I wipe the knife on the underside of my shirt and sheath it once again at my ankle. I'm proficient with this particular hunting knife; it's been a constant companion of mine for a while now, and I trust it to do its job well.

Today was no different. I walk back toward my car, leaving the scene with not so much as one drop of blood spilling out onto the pavement. In fact, I'm certain no one even heard me.

I'm quite proud of that.

And he never saw it coming. Too good of a death for him if you ask me—not enough suffering—but I can't be a part of those kinds of things any longer. I have to get on with my life.

If anyone glances over at him, he will just look like he tipped his head back for a long afternoon nap. By the time anyone notices, Penny and I will be well out of the area.

He was new to the distractor ways, probably born to it days before. He didn't have his full strength yet, not that that would even matter. I can take on a full-blown distractor any day of the week, but that would have made things more messy and attracted more attention.

I saved the family ahead of me, I know I did, and I take great comfort in that. The crazy thing is, I don't even care anymore if I catch on fire. I know I did the right thing; why should I be punished for it?

There have been times in this long life of mine that I have experienced horrendous things. If I intervene too much in a person's life, particularly a human, I will catch on fire. In other words, I *sponta-neously combust*. But you know what the worst thing is? It doesn't even kill me. But I do have to hide, and find a quiet place for a few hours, away from prying eyes. A secluded body of water is best.

I never suffer any ill effects. In fact, once the fire has left my body, I show no signs of being burned at all. In fact, I don't even have so much as a blister. I know, it's crazy. But that is my life. This curse was put upon me from my maker long ago, my punishment for intervening. But it didn't happen today.

Maybe the man upstairs is getting rusty with my comings and goings. I know he is busy, but he tends to forget the daily burdens of living, not to mention the constant annoyance of dealing with humanity.

They say not to carry grudges, but how can I not? This goes without saying, but it's not pleasant to be on fire. Sometimes, I feel like he quite enjoys my suffering. I wouldn't know; he doesn't talk to me.

But on this day, for whatever reason, I am not on fire, and I am grateful. I know I completely altered that family's life—and with good reason—and I feel nothing but good about that.

Penny has seen me on fire. It last happened twenty years ago, and I can recall every detail of that experience like it was yesterday. An experience like that has a way of sticking with a person.

Before I catch on fire, I usually get vertigo. Then the tingling sensations start—first in my limbs then it spreads throughout my body until it eventually takes over, and it's all I can feel. The tingling is replaced with heat, similar to how I imagine one might feel before passing out. Then the actual fire comes.

On that day twenty years ago, once I felt the tingling start, I knew I had about an hour before the fire would be running through me completely. I used that time to explain to Penny what was about to happen.

Given that she is well-acquainted with the supernatural and its ways, she took this bit of news pretty well, and she even helped me set up a plan. We decided I should hang out in our cellar full of potatoes that day while the fire raged through me—it was the only place we could think of where I could stay inconspicuous. It's dark and cool in our basement, and we have an oversized steel bathtub that she filled to the brim with water as cold as she could get it.

I still burn when I'm in the water, but the coolness helps take away a good amount of the sting. To this day, I take comfort in knowing she did that for me.

As we get closer to Neelsville, I smell peculiar things in the air. I don't care to make sweeping generalizations, but I'm certain that at least a third of Neelsville's residents and those in the surrounding areas are infected. I can smell it on them when I enter any store in the area.

I know better than to frequent the bars here. A new distractor drinking alcohol is quite dangerous.

Even as I drive through town, hoping to avoid trouble, I constantly see the ghosts of people I could have helped. The people on that bridge, for instance, oh so many years ago. It's always the first image that comes to mind when the guilt springs up. I helped so little in that calamity, and the few things I did do on that horrible day were not near enough. And it haunts me.

As does the reason I'm still walking around in the first place. I long to be free of this burden.

The only one who tempers this frustration is my dear Penny. She is my saving grace, and I love her more than life itself. She has always been in tune to this whole thing—who I am and what my purpose is here—but I'm worried for her. She has taken all this to heart.

She has abilities of her own. I've always known this about her; it's what drew me in. So I don't understand why she wants to come back here, but I don't question it. I'm sure she has her reasons.

Something else is bugging me about this town, too. A strange, rippling pattern floats in the air. I've seen this a handful of times over the many years that I have been alive—it's similar to a mirage or the heat coming off a gas grill. Invisible to the human eye, but still apparent.

I can see it just inside Neelsville's border, as soon as we enter the town. It's a telltale sign that someone in the area has manipulated time.

Which means there are distractors nearby. But a run-of-the-mill distractor cannot do this sort of thing. Only true evil can manipulate the order of things, especially time. I go through the laundry list of creatures I've met over the years that could accomplish something like this. I've met a good amount of them, but there's one name that keeps topping the list.

The demagogue, *Avalone.*

I had hoped that I was done dealing with him, but he's the irritating rash that never goes away. And I should have anticipated his strength. He can withstand a great many things, so of course he would be lurking about in these corners, peddling his darkness to the good residents of Neelsville. Invading it like a cancer and disguising himself as a piece of confetti. And I know he will not be satisfied until every good soul here has been turned.

And I'm not going to let this happen! Not if I can help it.

When time is manipulated, the aberration changes the course of every living thing near and far. Even plants in the ground are affected, since they depend so much on sunshine, specific times of the year, and the phases of the moon to grow and thrive. This is why I need to rid this place completely of them.

They are a pestilence that won't go away.

From what I know about distractors, they cannot manipulate *significant* amounts of time, just a few minutes here and there. It's why a person can look at a clock and not remember where the last few minutes have gone, which is not uncommon, it's the natural pull of time.

But on occasion, time is moved in an unnatural state, a hiccup, if you will. And it's the distractors that are manipulating it.

I turn into the short driveway of our rental and smile. Penny and I are renting a spacious cabin off of Highway 51. It sits nicely by the lake, and I love being here, just the two of us. The cabin is small compared to our usual accommodations, but I don't mind it. I enjoy being cooped up with her more than anything else in the world.

I don't care to socialize, either. When I go out, I tend to get asked too many prying questions, and I don't have the patience like I used to.

I spend a good portion of my evenings sitting on my dock, reflecting on my long life. I like being near water, and fishing makes me happy. I'm just a much better version of myself when I fish, however temporary that feeling may be.

Right now, I'm watching the sun set itself into the lake. I've seen this thousands of times, and I never tire of it.

But tonight, even with the comfort of the setting sun and the sounds of the lake, I still feel off. I can feel ripple sensations in the air. They are around us, these distractors, and they're hiding amongst the trees.

No matter how much I'd love to ignore it, I have to get these people prepared. Because this can't be ignored.

Something evil is coming.

THE MEETING

Lyle

Lyle watches as Margie pours him another shot. He finishes it in one gulp and takes a long look out over the lake. Things are churning once again in Neelsville. And when that starts to happen, things have a way of turning goofy downright fast.

First, he saw that thing on Carver island which he has told no one about and never will. From there, strange events trickled down like dominoes. Since Ethel's murder, the peculiar and strange appear to be hovering around every corner.

He came to Neelsville years ago to get away from this sort of nonsense, but now the crap storm is coming to him. He wants to wash his hands of it, really, but instead he keeps getting pulled in. Because of all this, things inside him are waking up.

"I'm afraid for our town," Margie said. "It's time we do something about it."

"I am, too, Margie." He motions for another drink. "I didn't want anything to do with this."

Margie grabs a beer mug from behind the bar—she knows him well enough to know what he'd like next—and sets it in front of him. "Well, we're knee-deep in kimchi now. We're in it whether or not we want to be."

She fills the mug to the brim, and Lyle takes a sip.

"I can keep these things off our tail only for so long. They're getting bolder. Yesterday, I had one in here for a good two hours telling me how much he liked to fish and that he bought a new place on the water up near Newaygo. He was fishing all right, but not for the swimming kind. He was looking for info."

"Newaygo?" Lyle shakes his head. "Crap, they're infiltrating our town like a disease."

Margie sniffs her agreement. "I knew he was making it up; I could smell the lie all over him. You know that poor kid who died last month on that motorcycle?"

Lyle nods. Kinda hard to forget an incident like that. The kid had been his next-door neighbor for years. Dewey could be a real pain in the ass—always climbing into his trees, throwing apples at random people, acting like a monkey at the zoo. Didn't have a lick of sense, but that never stopped Lyle from liking him. Now he would never be climbing trees again.

"Dewey didn't die getting hit by a car—he was murdered by that customer. I could hear his thoughts, and believe me, they weren't at all pleasant. Had me sick in the bathroom for hours afterward. I don't know about you, but I get the shivers just thinking about all these things coming here. I didn't think that was supposed to happen in a town like this."

"It wasn't. I thought that once they figured us out, they were going to leave. Supernatural creatures needing their own space and all."

"You think these things care much about protocol?" She shakes her head. "Anyway, I will reach out to the people I know, see what they think. Then we'll all have to figure out what to do."

Margie glances behind his head just as Lyle hears the door open, bringing the smell of the supernatural in along with a gust of warm air. Lyle smirks. Usually, those things keep their scent under wraps, but not today.

He wonders why as he sees Cassie wander up to the bar, ready for some day drinking. She glances around as she does, her eyes lighting up on each member of the group around her. "Oh Christ—we having a meetin'?"

Over the last few weeks, Lyle noticed that Cassie has been ratcheting up on her drinking. But for now he didn't want to think about it—there were more important matters at hand. But he's worried about her. He knows his group will be fine—and Cassie can usually handle her spirits—but if things go sideways again, they could use another good supernatural.

He glances around him, spying Crazy John at the far end of the bar. He was one of Margie's regulars, but he's just too clueless. And not to mention, one of the biggest mouths in Neelsville, so, he's out.

He watches as Crazy John eyeballs his plate of fish and chips. Given the glazed look in his eyes, a bomb could go off two feet away from him and he wouldn't even notice.

Margie lowers her voice as she leans in. "We need to be careful here; these things mean business. They don't give a rat's ass about anybody. What are we gonna do?"

Crazy John shouts from down the bar. "Can you believe this damn rain? It's like a cow pissin on a flat rock..every..damn...day!"

Most things that come out of Crazy John's mouth are gibberish, so Lyle pays him no mind. But then he spares a glance John's way and cringes. The man has the most annoying mustache in the world. It hangs a good half inch over his lip, and Lyle can't help but wonder what collected there over the course of the week. He fights the urge to trim it with Margie's bar scissors.

"Got some tartar sauce for this? And some white vinegar, too? Crap, I'm gonna need a fork. Christ, what kind of outfit you runnin' here?"

"Want me to eat it for you, too, John?" Margie finds the bottles of tartar sauce and vinegar and slides them across the bar. She reaches behind the bar and tosses something next to his plate. The distinctive sound of metal against ceramic echoes through the bar. "And here's your fork."

He glares at the utensil as he snatches it up. "Really, Margie? The tines on this are all bent. Looks like your dogs, Adam and Eve, were chewing on it."

"Well, bend it back, fella—I don't have time for this."

John flicks the lid off the vinegar and sprinkles a generous amount over the top of his sandwich.

"Take it easy, John."

"No easy about it; you know how I like my sauces."

"And you're the only one I know who eats it that way."

Margie sneers and finishes wiping down the counter. She likes keeping things orderly in her bar.

A few more customers walk in, one being Bruce. Margie looks surprised to see him, and Lyle doesn't blame her. He rarely comes in— Lyle hasn't seen him in a coon's age.

"Hey, buddy," Margie calls from behind the bar as he shuffles up.

His shoulders are hunched over. "Shot of whiskey."

Margie grabs a bottle and pours him a glass. "What brings you in today?"

He takes a long sip then slams the glass down. "It's a bar, isn't it?"

Lyle senses someone else behind him, so he turns, spying a man wearing a long brown overcoat who's carrying himself in an almost regal manner. His eyes look like they hold an ocean of secrets, and Lyle can't remember the last time he saw him in here. The man defines the word "mysterious."

Margie's eyes brighten as she calls out to him. "You there! Wow, it sure has been awhile! I can't remember the last time you've stepped foot in my bar."

His eyebrows furrow. "Do I need a permit?"

"No permit needed, darlin'." She grins.

Lyle can tell Margie's trying to mind her own business, but he knows she's fishing for information. Cassie's curious, too, apparently. His wife's head is twisted completely around, staring the stranger down like a snake would size up a mouse. Any minute now, Cassie will be openly vocalizing her opinion of this man. Lyle shifts in his seat at the thought. He didn't want her scaring him off, he looked like he might have some answers.

He takes a seat at the bar, glancing around. The silence lengthens to the point of awkwardness before Margie pipes up. "I'm sorry, sir. It's just that, well, you usually keep to yourself."

He smiles politely as he sips his drink.

"Say, you got that place a few miles down near Bevard's, that big cabin up there on the river, right?" Cassie asks. "You are one lucky son of a bitch to have that."

The man eyes Cassie up and down. He looked both interested and irritated at the same time. Lyle would know—it's part of her charm.

"Yes, I'm one lucky 'son of a bitch,' as you call it." Lyle noticed that he thought her comment to be funny.

"You'll have to excuse my wife," Lyle offers. "She was born with a big mouth."

The man waves a dismissive hand, "No worries."

Lyle scrutinizes the man more closely. Maybe he can get this guy into their little "supernatural" club. Something about him seems trustworthy and likable. Never mind that he's known him for about five minutes.

"It has come to my attention that things in this town are not what they appear to be."

Crazy John, Lyle, Cassie, Margie, and Bruce all lean in.

"My wife has told me of such things, and I tend to listen to her. Now I know there are strange things here, and we have to decide how were going to deal with them."

"Penny! That's right, you're married to Penny. I see that doll in the grocery store every so often. She used to stay at Fish-A-While when she was younger. Oh, isn't she quite something?"

"She sure is. Anyway, I would like to help with whatever is going on around here. I feel bad after that murder."

Cassie brushes away tears. "Ethel was my best friend."

The man nods as if he knows that. Hell, for all Lyle knows, he does.

"Well, we all feel bad about Ethel. Penny knew her as well. My condolences."

Lyle eyes the stranger again. "I never caught your name."

"They call me, the Traveller."

"Oh, that's downright interesting. How did you go about getting that name?" Cassie asks.

"Sort of something that stuck over the years, mam."

Cassie's eyes scan him up and down. "So, you're not gonna tell us your real name? You gonna be all Mr. Incognito?"

Cassie's just being flirty, but Lyle knows that's just her way.

As the conversation shifts, Lyle considers their options. He watches the group as they talk. Bruce keeps inserting helpful tips into the conversation, so Lyle knows he's on the right track.

He's been itching to get Bruce into their group. He knows it would be a good call. Bruce emanates good energy, and he's strong, too.

But he would let the others figure that out. The only thing Lyle knows about Bruce is that he drives a school bus for a living, and on occasion, would wander into Margie's bar looking out of sorts. It was his usual look, which was a sad thing to see.

And Lyle was all too familiar with it. He's been there. Last year, there were many times that he was so depressed that he couldn't even get out of bed.

And it started soon after he saw that thing.

ORIGINS

The Traveller

*I*t's been thousands of years, and I can still remember the exact shade of his cloth. Of all the regrets a person can have in this world, mine is by far the worst: to see humanity in all its pursuits, to notice all its earthly pleasures and sins. It's an arduous burden, but bear it, I must.

My mind forever reeling over the accounts of that day. How he must have felt when getting beaten and spit on. The humiliation and isolation, the utter desolation, the slaughter. This event sits with me constantly, always in the back of my mind, and I can think of little else. *It is a torture.*

I remember it like it was yesterday. I was standing amidst a crowd, and he understood my plan with a mere glance in my direction. I wasn't even worthy of it, or the bitterness of his words, really—I know that now—but he gave them to me anyway. I see him and his last words everywhere I go. *I can see them in my dreams.* How could I not? Every night, I see the toil and strain in his face, the muted brown of his bloodshot eyes, his last gaze that made me wish I had died that day right along with him.

The day my soul changed forever.

And the shame never leaves me. It's a disease, spilling out of my every pore. I can barely tolerate living in my own skin, and the weariness has settled into my veins like a brick. Gone is the vigor of life.

My misfortune is not unknown to animals, either; they all sense my lifelong script. In fact, all living things on this earth are privy to my affliction, and they know it as soon as I come into view.

Other sentient beings know it, too. It's the fickle humans that seem oblivious to my plight.

And yet, the world still turns, doesn't it? However hollow it may be, and my heart still beats, however broken.

The behavior of humans is the one constant that I know. They wander around like sheep, half asleep in their pitiful young lives, growing old and never awakening to their true potential—what they could be—out of fright or pity or God knows what else. Well, that's just not living.

I so wish I could tell them. They are walking corpses going after the wrong things, making the wrong decisions, getting connected with the wrong people, and they repeat it over and over again. A rather vile way to live out one's life.

And who am I? I could be the neighbor walking down the street inviting someone over for coffee (though I wouldn't, I don't care for mindless chit chat). I'm the cook in the pizzeria or the postman delivering the mail. One can walk past me and never look twice—I wear the mask of normalcy, and I've played the part well.

In truth, I have roamed this earth for thousands of years. But I'm getting tired of roaming, and death is all I long for now. My family lineage died off long ago.

City life, island life, sleeping-out-in-the-desert life—I've done it all. And believe me, I would welcome the bite of the pit viper snake if that would do me in. But I know it wouldn't. Even as my body would fill up with the toxin, I would still rise to see another day.

For I am just going through the motions. Everything is just an act; I'm not really alive but a mere shell of a man.

I can still hear the soft whispers from an echoing demon. Those dirty words echo in my ear like a haunting lullaby: *You will never be enough, you piece of garbage.*

It will always be this way, and no matter how much I want to forget, I can't. It's a movie that plays over and over in the recesses of my mind—with the same disgusting ending, every time.

))

They are all taunting him, the man with the wooden slab of a cross weighing heavily across his back. Meanwhile, the monstrous and the fickle are standing around him in their little crowds, laughing hysterically one minute, screaming the next. Their brains polluted with excess and lust, and the energy of the crowd pecking away at him like scavengers on a hunt.

He has bruises on top of bruises, blood-stained hair, and bloody streaks running down his legs and onto his toes. The blood is everywhere—his body is covered in a blanket of cuts and scratches with no sandals on his feet. Not that sandals would help at this point; his toes are mangled and bloodied, and the bottoms of his feet are black.

A defeated man. And I'm right here, witnessing it all.

It has finally come to this, a man being torn to shreds. Everyone is caught up in the thrill of seeing something like that up close, the utter desecration of a human being. There's a sick fascination to it.

That's when I say, "Hurry up; get on with it."

And in return, he glances back at me and responds, *"And you will wait here until I come back."*

How I wish I didn't say those words, but I just can't bear the sight of this anymore. I want it to be over.

))

When is he coming back? No one really knows the answer. Meanwhile, here I sit, trying to stop that tricky devil called time. To think that I have what most people dream of.

I get to—well, *have to*—wander the earth, partake in its adventures. And I will do this until the end of time—or until the redeemer comes back, whichever happens first. By my calculations, I may still be waiting another hundred years, perhaps thousands. I really have no idea. I don't know when he is coming back, I'm not privy to that information.

I do know one thing, though: Time is a beast.

I have no real friends. Well, not in the last millennium or two. Yet my mind remembers every significant person I've encountered, every soul I've ever loved.

My eyes remember everything, too, and my breath is a continual sigh. I want relief, but it never comes.

I'm a walking archive, a folly, an absurd trinket, the ever-decaying fixture, except . . . I don't decay. My never-ending benefit of good health is simply a reminder of how I long to simply be struck down.

I want another chance at redemption.

I've prayed for this over and over so many times, and yet, I am never granted an answer. Perhaps whoever I'm praying to is fast asleep.

I've seen too many things in this long life of mine. Strange serpents in the sea, crazy lights in the sky, curious objects flying about in the evening—all enough to make the strongest of men squirm.

From the depths of the ocean, I saw a host of these mysterious things. I once served in the military and lived in a submarine. I discovered that there are things in the sea that no one likes to talk about. Any seafaring man can tell you this, but I can't share in my wisdom. The few times I made this mistake, my body was on fire for twenty-four hours. That was my punishment.

So, I found my way to water to alleviate the pain. For though I can still feel the flames underwater, the burning is a bit muted. I learned then that I can stay underwater for up to an hour. Thankfully, it helped with the pain.

Despite these burdens—or perhaps because of their frequency—I often look for interesting ways to pass the time. I've gotten quite good at being inconspicuous and role playing. It's the only good thing about being immortal.

I've had many different vocations over the years.

I was once a cobbler, a candlestick maker, and a medicine man. I was there during the Black Plague on a ship bound for Florence. The rat-infested ship was a mass of floating disease, macabre and smelly. To this day, I don't care to ride on the ocean—it doesn't matter how big the boat is. I can still taste the vomit, and feel the stinging spray of the sea. The groans of the sick and dying were all around me, and there was no hiding from it.

Well, that's not exactly true. I did try.

I once jumped off the deck of a perfectly good ship. I was hoping to drown, but it was futile. Every few decades, I like to test out my immortality, to see if anything has changed.

It never does.

I always end up floating up to the surface. I'd hoped that maybe a sea monster could do me in back then. I'd heard rumors of a monster that swam in those waters and would eat anything that fell into them. A man from our boat had even fallen overboard and was killed this way, and he'd only been in the water a few minutes. I guess even the creatures of the sea are in on my dirty little secret.

Apparently, doomed souls are left alone.

My flesh does not taste good to them anyway. The animals have told me this. In fact, my flesh does not taste good to any living thing on this earth.

But I digress.

I once tried my hand at being a 16th-century poet. Ah, this century also saw the birth of arguably one of the finest poets of the English language, William Shakespeare. Interestingly enough, we both ran in the same circles. He was fascinated with the spiritual realm, the true belief that the body and spirit were perpetually connected, he wrote poems about this very thing. He always tried mingling the real with the unreal, fascinated with the metaphysical. Poets write about this all the time, and we both took that particular topic on. I didn't get particularly famous, but he sure did. He was a shiny spot in my otherwise droll existence during that time.

I was a schoolteacher in the 1950s. God, I hated the way they talked back then. Everything was either "nifty" or "square"—add to that all the grease in their hair, the poodle skirts, the sock hops . . . good grief. But I have to say, there was something about that time that was just so well, innocent. I can't help but smile when I think about it. People weren't as jaded—in fact, they were downright childlike.

I taught history during that time. I soon found out that young people have an infuriating way of frying my brain. I only hope that I proved to be useful in their education.

I was a bridge builder in the 1960s. Of all the jobs I'd had, that one was the most memorable by far. Whenever I think of bridges, my mind recalls the traumatic events of the most famous bridge collapse in history, oh so long ago. And I was there—along with a fantastic grouping of others.

For months before the event, I watched in vain as myself and a few scant others tried to give the humans various signs. Since I am super-natural, I knew what was coming, and I didn't want any innocents to be killed. The others didn't much care. They regarded humans in much the same way as a human might regard an insect.

My thoughts drift to that daft, young fellow that I tried to help. I couldn't get through to him; his stubbornness was as hard as a coffin nail. But I had to try. I knew he was going to be traveling on that bridge on that particular evening—I read it in his mind. I knew, down to the last second, when it would be collapsing into the river.

But he just wouldn't listen. I messed with his car, trying to stop him from crossing that bridge. I wanted to give him a little extra time to change his mind.

That's the problem with humans: They don't pay attention to things around them, even when the signs are smacking them in the face. They think they know everything, that they're invincible, and that couldn't be further from the truth.

I found myself becoming so emotionally attached that I almost caught on fire again. I made the mistake of manifesting right in front of him, telling him exactly what was going to happen. He started screaming at me, saying I was a lunatic, insisting that I leave him alone.

Maybe my eyes looked strange in that moment—I can't control their color if I'm passionate about something. Whether they were or not, the young man never listened to me, and his stubbornness cost him his life that awful day.

The collapse happened in 1968, during the height of the Christmas season, and people were busy, out doing their shopping. A cable had snapped on one of the suspension bridges, causing it to crumble into the water. The bridge had been packed full of traffic—and this was all preplanned.

There had been very suspicious sightings of UFOs and reports of weird creatures paying visits to people in the surrounding neighborhoods. This is all true. When evil comes at this magnitude, it awakens every living thing around it. This includes other creatures. Everything is *curious*. But the humans know nothing of this, the most they can surmise is that people are crazy.

But there had been one woman. Just one.

She'd been frequenting my favorite diner, one that sat a couple of blocks from the bridge and with the most stunning view of the river. She would often come in the mornings, looking like a lost angel, while ordering her coffee. I would watch as she stared out the window at the bridge, and scribbled things down in her journal. I often wondered what she could be writing so intently about, but I liked that she came every morning to do it.

I could see that she was well-versed in the "shining" or clairvoyance, or whatever people liked to call it these days. I had seen it on her straight away, her inner chakra saturated with the wondrous and the odd.

I supposed she was having a hard time with it—I watched as it clung to her like a lost child, surrounding her like a warm blanket. I wished she could have seen it, but a person cannot see their own aura.

Over the years, I have managed to get plenty of other innocent people killed. Funny though, God tends to protect the fools and the drunkards. I have no idea why, but I've seen it consistently enough, that I'm convinced of this theory's credence.

I remember what she ordered on the day of the bridge collapse, it was a cup of coffee and a piece of rhubarb pie. She liked her coffee black, but that day she'd poured two packets of sugar in it. I guess she wanted some sweetening up.

Remembering mundane details are the bane of my existence, but with her, I want to know all of them. In fact, I ache for them. That's how I knew she was the one.

I watched that day as she swirled her spoon around, staring at that beautiful view of the bridge, unaware of her own beauty.

And she was a beauty. Her auburn hair cascaded down her shoulders like a rich waterfall. It always looked windblown, like someone shook her hard before she walked out of the house. I could tell that she didn't care much about what she wore because her shirts were always wrinkled. I didn't give a damn; it was a big part of why I liked her.

She seemed transfixed on that bridge, and it was then that I noticed a moment of heavy realization spread across her face like a dark shadow.

She knows.

At first, I thought I was just seeing things. But all I could do is stare, wide-eyed, as the steady flow of epiphany washed over her like a rogue river. It was poetry to witness, and I found my heart had started racing. Finally, someone, so slight and unassuming, was experiencing a little bit of what I had to go through every day. I wanted to celebrate, jump up and down. Heck, I wanted to buy everyone in that diner a meal.

I didn't do that, of course, but I *did* do something that I hadn't done in a long time. I called the waitress over so I could look at the menu. And you know what I did after that?

I actually ordered food.

This is rare; because I don't really need it. The only thing I require to survive is water, and even then, I can go vast amounts of time without it.

But good heavens, I actually wanted to order something off the menu! How long had it been since I had a meal? I tried to remember, but I couldn't even recall the last thing I ate. I was thinking it could have been some sort of soup.

I do eat once in a while, just to make sure I can still chew. I know there's a certain pleasure to be derived from eating, but in my usual depressive state, I can't tell.

How much time had passed since I felt anything prior to that day? I didn't even know—it was embarrassing, really. But suddenly, in that diner, I recognized it: feelings for her. Maybe.

But I didn't even know her. Who was she to me? She was nothing, and yet . . .

I glance again at the menu, thinking I would order a BLT. Good lord, they better not screw it up by putting on Miracle Whip. I'll even flirt with the waitress a bit, ask her what the special was. This mysterious women was waking things up in me that I didn't know existed.

It didn't seem like she had many friends or anyone to confide in. And I knew what that was like, I've always been thought of as an outcast. That had been my tribe—until I became a tribe of one.

I offer a silent prayer to the heavens, wrenching my thoughts back to the present. *Oh, how I hate living this way. Please, if there is a higher being, please let me make this right. I want to make it right so badly. Just tell me what I need to do.*

As my thoughts drift back to those poor, lost souls at the bridge, and I wonder what part they had to play in all this? What a sick ending to a story.

Sometimes, when I close my eyes, all I can see are those bloody packages, floating about in the water. Water-soaked gifts drifting down to the bottom of that lake where car engines still ran, and headlights still shone.

I can still hear the banging on windows, and the rays of headlights casting haunting shadows down at the bottom. I tried to get as many out as I could, but I couldn't reach everyone. But I am thankful for the few lucky souls that managed to swim to shore without so much as a scratch.

Hell was brought to that town that day, and it would never be the same. From then on, during the Christmas season, everyone can sense the malaise in the air, it surrounds the town like a putrid pestilence. Leftover thoughts of those that had perished. A lingering shadow that's never appropriately addressed.

Around the holidays, homeowners find themselves closing their windows and keeping themselves hidden away, and scratching their heads while doing so. What should be a festive time becomes over-whelming and full of anxiety.

The farther a person drives out of town, the more the feeling dissi-pates, until it disappears entirely.

I've always felt that I could have done more. A bunch of us had migrated there as observers because there was talk of a planned disas-ter. And it all started with an arbitrary trinket.

Imagine that. A major disaster caused by the most minor, uncal-culating, inanimate thing: a screw.

Bridges require constant care in order to function properly, but they also require a lot of money to maintain. To the untrained eye, the bridge collapse was almost inevitable.

But an act of malevolence can start in the most innocuous of ways. Add to that the simple passage of time, and you get the beginnings of a ghoulish recipe.

Once these two issues were decided, the supreme beings had to figure out what bridge they wanted to destroy.

I attended hours of meetings on this very subject. I remember this heinous lot sitting around, sipping on their eccentric drinks, and smok-ing their acrid cigars. For supreme beings, they sure enjoyed all the vices that humankind had to offer. They were a collection of motley demons, enjoying the spoils of decadence and gluttony.

I was in attendance in these meetings more than I care to count. I still feel guilty about it.

The discussions centered around the selection of the unlucky bridge. They wanted it to be, and I quote: "a most impressive showing of evil."

First, they narrowed the options down to suspension bridges. I remember their insidious laughter that rang out as one of those evil things started detailing how this was all going to go down.

I remember as the demon thing took in a puff of smoke stating, "What an extravagant accident!"

They, of course, wanted the collapse to be as destructive as possible, and, according to them, a suspension bridge would be perfect.

Their first choice was the Golden Gate Bridge in San Francisco. One of the most famous bridges in the world, and, at the time of its construction, the world's longest suspension bridge.

But in the end, they decided not to go with that one. They zeroed in on a suspension bridge in Ohio. It was built in the twenties, and *long* overdue for maintenance and upkeep. The problem was, the town did not have the money for things like that; most young towns don't.

And it's always about the money, isn't it? Everything dark usually is.

From there, they discussed how it would happen and when. They all agreed that it would be most effective—and harmful—during the Christmas season.

Over the years, I've run into all kinds of strange beings, but those things were of a different breed entirely, and I don't care to meet them again.

December 1968

The Traveller

J think I might befriend the young women sitting in the corner
booth. I don't see the harm in at least introducing myself. I feel
that an effort should be made, since now she's caught me on
more than one occasion staring at her.

I've learned that my fire only starts if I reveal things to a human
that I shouldn't. So over the many centuries, I've learned what's okay
to talk about and what to avoid.

I've had friends over the years, but I usually have to leave before
they start getting suspicious about my, well, *situation*. Usually, it
takes around sixteen years—give or take a year—when things start
to unravel.

If I'm friends with someone for longer than fifteen years, the
nature of the friendship inevitably starts to change. Questions get
asked, and I'm left to come up with rather elaborate reasons of why I
haven't aged. I usually go with the standard "good genes," "sunscreen
is your friend," "vitamins," "exercise," blah, blah, blah.

My last true friend couldn't get over the fact that I hadn't had any wrinkles. Over beers one afternoon, he kept prodding me on the subject, asking me what my secret really was, and I just laughed it off. Of course, he wouldn't let the subject drop. As he was finishing his beer, assessing me, his eyes had widened, and a strange realization came over his face.

I decided then that it was time for me to go. It was better for the both of us in the long run. I didn't want to kill my friend for figuring it out nor did I want to catch on fire by saying too much. But I really hated having to drop that friendship; he was a funny guy.

Sometimes, on occasion, I will run into someone that I knew forty or fifty years prior. You would think after crisscrossing continents over several millennia, that it would be difficult to run into someone I knew, but alas, the world is indeed smaller than one would think.

I've had several close calls in this regard. I sometimes don't take into account that others travel, too. Blame it on ego or foolishness, but I really should have known better.

I've had this happen with lovers too.

One afternoon, I had been riding a bike along a pleasant little patch of coastline that didn't suck. It was a better-than-average day. Then out of the blue, it was like the devil himself had snapped his fingers, causing a trail of chaos. A dog had ran out in front of me.

That damn dog ruined everything. He caused me to swerve, and I couldn't gain back my control, so I ended up hitting the pavement pretty hard. My friend, who had seen the whole thing, insisted I go to the doctor.

While insisting that I was fine—repeatedly—she noticed the marks on my arms and leg where I fell.

We were sitting outside a café, and she wouldn't stop staring at my arm, asking about my scratches over and over again.

We had a good argument over that one. I told her she was making a big deal out of nothing, and she stated that she knew what she saw, and that she wasn't going crazy.

We parted ways shortly after that. Her goodbye excuse was that I made her uncomfortable. Maybe that was in her best interest. I couldn't quite blame her, but it did make me sad.

Did she ever really love me if that scared her off? Wasn't love supposed to conquer all?

I'm immortal, which means I must be some kind of monster, right? And how can I ever expect a human to come to terms with that?

I'd thought by now that I would have run into someone else like me, but nope. *Apparently, I'm the only screwup in history that talked out of turn and was cursed forever for it.*

And I have yet to meet a human immortal.

So, I don't really see anything wrong with starting a conversation. I can ask why she buries her face in a journal every day. What's the harm in that?

I walk over to her, and she smiles. I sit down in her booth, and when she doesn't tell me to leave, I just stare. I'm fascinated by her.

"What is your name?" Her eyes dance as she answers. "I'm Penny."

From that moment on, I am transfixed.

MARCUS RETURNS

Brooke

I awaken to the sound of soft rain hitting my window. I stare up at the ceiling, wondering how this day is going to pan out. I look out the window and see a swirling mass of grey clouds; *situation normal.* Just another stormy day here in Neelsville.

All this gray, rain and thunder only underlines the way I'm feeling.

Way off in the distance, I see Cassie sitting on her dock. I noticed the other day she was back to wearing her heavy makeup, as per usual. But it was good to see her getting back to her usual self, even with the added foundation.

I sure hope that's what she's doing, and I wonder if Scout is a nice diversion for her.

Maybe she's turning a corner in dealing with Ethel's death. I didn't think she ever would. Though it isn't, of course, without the help of pills and alcohol.

I sit up in bed, thinking about Cassie's inner pain, and wondering about my own. It's been months since I've seen or heard anything from Aaron.

Where are you? And why aren't you coming back?

I have to remind myself of the possibility that maybe he changed his mind, and decided to stay in his lands. I couldn't blame him, really; his whole family is there.

He may never be coming back.

Perhaps I had made something more of the relationship.

But I just can't get him out of my head.

As I stare out my window, I see my favorite tree. It's twisted up and crooked, and looks like something straight out of a fairy tale.

In that moment, I see an outline of someone standing next to it. I'm a bit shocked. He's tall and at first I think it was Aaron. I yell out.

Aaron?!

For a brief few seconds I think I might have conjured him. I jump out of bed, my heart pounding with the strange elation of excitement and fear. I realize than it's not Aaron.

It's Marcus.

The last time I saw Marcus, he had just finished killing Ethel. I'll always remember how his silvery blade caught the moonlight, and the vacant look in his eyes as he did so. Things I wish I could forget.

I swallow hard to steady myself as I watch him traverse the short path to my window.

He doesn't look very happy.

I see him forming the words "we need to talk," and my heart leaps up into my throat. I don't really want to talk to Marcus. I should've known this was coming. I feel like a kid about to be scolded.

I have *many* questions swirling around, but I try to act casual, beat him to the punch.

"Talk? Yeah, sure." I want to scream: *Where's Aaron?"*

Before I utter another word, Marcus enters my bedroom with lightning speed.

I don't have a good answer for how he got in. Just, one minute, he's at my window, the next, he's standing against my paisley pink curtains in my bedroom. Under different circumstances, I would find this funny. But his eyes look like they're about to burst.

"What's wrong?"

"They got him, Brooke."

What?! I feel the urge to throw up.

He stares at the floor, his cheeks flushed. "The distractors took him away a few weeks ago. I've been trying to track them down for the last forty-eight hours, but to no avail. I wanted to come tell you sooner, but I was holding out for some better news."

Marcus unable to outrun anything seemed impossible. "How could this happen?" I ask.

He eyes me as he takes in a deep breath. "I'm sure he told you about them, how we're not dealing with humans here. These beings are light years ahead of us, you know that right?"

"Well, you guys have powers, too!" I'm pleading, and I feel sick as hot tears flood down my cheeks. Of course, I know all this—I know what we're dealing with—I've seen it firsthand. My cheeks redden as I realize the truth: Marcus doesn't think I'm capable of anything.

He continues. "I'm sorry. I should have told you sooner, but I'd hoped to get a lead on him first. The last thing I wanted to do was come here with this kind of news."

"It's been weeks, Marcus," I bit back. "I thought you all were dead, that you guys just left."

"I know, and I'm truly sorry. He'd always planned to come back, warn you. But the distractors are all over this town, I'm afraid. Some of them were even at the funeral. I hate to say it, but it's not safe for you anymore."

"*You were at the funeral?* Why didn't you come see me?"

"Like I'm gonna show myself."

I lean forward, folding my arms across my chest. "Marcus, I've been worried! I had no idea where you guys were. I could have used a friend, at least."

He sighs. "It's not safe for me to be seen here, especially during the daytime. And it would be bad for you, too."

"Why?" I ask, but I already know his answer.

Neelsville has slowly been taken over.

My vision shrinks as the realization sinks in. Before the dizziness takes over, I feel a pair of strong arms jolt me back to awareness.

I find my voice. "I knew this was going to happen. He kept saying it wouldn't, but I knew it."

Marcus's hands squeeze my biceps. "Brooke, this isn't your fault. They eventually would have come anyway."

"But I'm the reason they got him. He said I attract their kind!"

I felt like a child then. But I needed to hear some answers.

Marcus's eyes droop as his shoulders fall, and lets out a loud sigh. "They're already here, Brooke. And they've been here for a while; they were just in disguise."

Horrible images of Aaron being tortured take over my mind, and I'm finding it hard to breathe. "*What are we gonna do? What are they going to do to him?*"

"I need you to listen to me." Marcus takes one of my hands in his. "Everything will work out."

"Yeah, okay," I shoot back, rolling my eyes. "We're at the end, and you think everything is fine."

"Listen to me, Brooke. I know everything isn't fine. But I *am* going to get him back. And they will *pay* for what they're doing."

Staring into his eyes, I really couldn't doubt him. His stare looked like he could penetrate my skull. And the green cast to his eyes looked like they were on fire.

God, he's intense.

"What do you want me to do?"

He nods once, relaxing his grip on my hand. "I want you to keep acting like nothing has happened."

"I've been doing that."

"But you need to continue! Go on about your business. And by God, do not tell anyone."

I've been keeping this sharp nugget of knowledge now for the last six months. I think I could hold out for longer.

"Defeating them is impossible alone, Marcus. We need more help! And this whole giant secret is getting harder to keep."

"I'm figuring it out. Just try to be strong. I do have an idea where they might be congregating, but I'll need your help."

I had this very conversation with Aaron only a few months ago, and I know what he's about to ask of me. I am going to be the bait. I know from Aaron's stories that distractors can smell Aaron's kind miles away—but a human can distract them.

"You know that doctor in town? Well, he's one of them."

"What? Are you sure?" I hiss.

"I noticed him at the funeral; it's all over him. I wanted to waste him right then, but there were too many people. Whatever you do, don't go near that damn med center. I suspect one of the nurses there is already one, too."

He finds my gaze. "This particular group can't be too far from here; I say fifty miles, tops. Not a lot of them, but there are a few. And they might even be prominent members of your town."

My stomach clenches, hating that this is all my fault.

"It isn't."

He's reading my mind. So be it. I just want Aaron back.

"You know that old windmill back in the woods?" he asks.

"Yes."

"We can communicate through that. If he has any messages, I'll be able to see it in there."

I cock my head to the side. "How the heck does that even work?"

"It's just something we can do." He sighs again. "Once I get my hands on at least one of them, I can get lots of intel. All I need is one."

I stand up and stare out at the surface of the lake. It looks like dark glass, full of secrets and mirrors and God knows what underneath. How is it that my peaceful home is suddenly a haven for supernatural monsters?

I couldn't believe the doctor. Funny, I never suspected him. It's sad, really—he seemed so nice.

How did I not detect that on him?

"He's not nice, Brooke. He could kill you right now, and he probably would!"

But he was so friendly and nice to me the other day.

Marcus takes a step closer, and I can feel his breath on my neck. I know he can sense my unease, and he's in full fighting mode. I take a step back, pressing myself up against the bedroom wall.

He follows. "Aaron is my brother."

"I know." I can't help but shake in his presence. And I just stand there like a dummy, wondering what he's thinking.

"Don't be afraid of me, Brooke."

But I am.

"I'm not."

That didn't sound too convincing. There are so many reasons to be afraid of Marcus, I couldn't even name them all.

I'm sure my fear is apparent on my face. I could never be a poker player. I recall then what Aaron said about Marcus being a warrior, and that he is one of their greats. Sure, he's dangerous; that's a given. But he doesn't have to be so smug about it.

He brushes my bangs aside, his hand large and strong. I'm sure he's aware that I'm trembling. "Are you sure you can do this?"

Of course, I can do this. I will do anything for Aaron. *Marcus* is the one unnerving me.

"Yes, I can."

He stares into my eyes. I don't know what he's looking for. Deception, perhaps? Well, when it comes to Aaron, I'm not capable of it.

He grabs my arm, and my eyes shoot to his. "Marcus?"

"Meet me tomorrow across the street. We'll find the trail into the woods, and from there, we will get to the bottom of this and find him."

I nod, hoping he'll let go of my arm. He holds onto it a few moments longer, and finally lets go. The man has too much testosterone for his own good, even if he is a supernatural being.

He senses my discomfort. "I will see you tomorrow, Brooke."

I watch as my long, sheer curtains graze at my wooden floors. The smell of Marcus is strong, and will probably linger in my room for a while.

Funny how all the members of Aaron's family like visiting me in my room. It would appear that once again, things are going to change for me.

DR. COOPER

Dr. Cooper

J have been waiting for this moment for a long time.

I'd heard rumblings from the higher-ups that when I came to Neelsville, I would be hitting a few snags. I just didn't expect it to be from her. But that is just the way of things, isn't it? Just when things start to fall into place, life has that irritating way of taking you off course.

I first saw her at the funeral. I couldn't help but notice the careful way she caressed her hair while standing in the rain. The slight dimple in her cheek—it had made its appearance now and then—in a delicate dance--especially when she found something funny. I liked the way she laughed as she was getting her plate at the buffet.

And I can't stop thinking about her.

She held my gaze here and there throughout the funeral, I only hope I wasn't too obvious. I didn't think I was. But with every new day, I am one step closer to becoming a distractor, and deceit becomes easier to me. You can cover up heaps of it with an engaging smile.

I could smell her in the air for the entire service, which made it hard to concentrate—much less pretend that I gave a damn about whoever it was for in the first place. And let's face it; it's not the easiest thing to pretend I'm sad when she's making my mouth water.

Since our brief encounter at the doctor's office, she's been constantly running through my mind.

It's always this way with me. When I want something, I fall fast and hard. And after seeing her for the second time at the clinic, my feelings for her have solidified.

I'm always good at making something out of nothing, because nothing is the only thing I've ever had. I can twist nothing around in the recesses of my brain until it becomes, well, *something*. And something I can work with, manifest it into reality.

At least I have that to look forward to.

Quite often the damage of my past will come tap me on the shoulder, telling me what I don't want to hear. And most times, I do need to hear it. But the anguish, the embarrassment, the desire—it's almost too much to bear. And when this happens, I usually run it off.

I don't know if I like yet what I've become. Funny, for most of my life I've worked hard, kept my nose to the grindstone, and achieved much in the medical community. You could almost call me a stellar citizen. And for what?

The beginning of the end started when my fiancée cheated. *Stupid bitch.*

I think back to my earliest days as a distractor. I had been in the medical profession all my grown life—and had always been ethical. Beaver Cleaver would have been proud. In fact, I was a born rule follower, a parent's dream, the perfect gentlemen.

And where had that gotten me? Nowhere, and with a broken heart.

Which only proves that even if you do everything right, things can still turn out half-baked and sideways. After all I've done, all those hard-working years of helping people, I still managed to become a joke.

It started when my girlfriend ran off with my best friend—such an embarrassing cliché—a bitter seed had been planted. I rarely let myself go to that awful place, it's filled with darkness and regret, and the anger is still fresh.

Grime sits there too. And if a person stays too long, it becomes a part of them.

Reminders of her are everywhere. When I pass by our favorite hole-in-the-wall restaurant on the way to work. When I drive down the street where we used to walk together to watch the sunset. Where had it all gone wrong, and how did I not see the signs?

It had been a particularly trying year. My mom, Helena, who pretty much raised me, had died of ovarian cancer. That same year is when my fiancée ran out of my life. What hurts the most is how easy it was for her to do it.

Well, I know it wasn't easy for my mom, she had no choice, but boy did she fight. I don't like to think about that too much. Her grave-stone, which I know is a bit over-the-top, is the only thing I have left of her. I'd picked the most expensive one, and of course, with the most elaborate font. When I visit—which is often—I always make sure the grass around her grave is clear of pesky weeds. She always liked peonies, so I make sure there are some in full view, fake or otherwise.

In the face of this loss, I can understand the lure of it, the lure of becoming a distractor.

I was never good at navigating friendships. Often, when I did put in the effort, it never panned out—I just didn't have the time. Medical school had been my entire existence; endless hours of rotation, with endless lives to save.

And now I can barely stand my own reflection. This may change, they said it would, I guess I just need to wait a few more weeks.

My heart rate is running fast this morning, and I feel like someone poured rocket fuel into my veins. *I have to run this off.*

I throw on some gym clothes and step out my front door. The first few blocks are easy peasy—I have so much adrenaline, and feel punchy from the night before. And it isn't from alcohol.

Christ, I can't even run without thinking about her. This is ridiculous.

I turn off Sherman Road and head east—not my usual route, but the lure of the lake and the woods is strong; I guess I need nature in larger doses today. I let the warmth of the sunshine soak into my pours. God bless the sun—it has a way of making life more tolerable.

I'm just starting to hit my stride when the runner's high kicks in. One of the best things in the world,—well, that and Brooke Larkin.

During these times, I often think of what I had with my ex-girl-friend, quite a lifetime ago. But these feelings are so buried, I almost feel powerless when they rise up in me, spilling out into my current life at awkward times. There were many times in the ER that I almost lost it. I take pity on the nurse that I yelled at now. She was only doing her job.

I hate that I can't control this anger.

Hopefully this will dissipate once I become full-blown distractor. I am now one of the most powerful beings on earth. How could I ever think of a human in this way, and why would I even want to? I couldn't explain it—*I just knew how I felt.*

As I think of Brooke now, I feel desire come on like a freight train.

Get a hold of yourself!

I run back to the house and into the bathroom. I fill up the sink and hold my face under, letting the coolness of the water sink into my skull, wishing it would numb my existence.

I lift up out of the water, my face pink and dripping, and stare at the face in the mirror.

I hardly recognize myself. I do see the sinister becoming more apparent. It plays itself across my face like I've placed a gray, translucent shadow on top of it.

I first noticed these changes last week, and I'm kinda digging it. Muscles are coming out of the woodwork, too. That's a nice perk, since my work doesn't really allow time for workouts.

I'm lucky I got in a run today. I was hoping the change of scenery would let me forget her for a while. But of course, that plan was doomed from the start.

Or maybe my last shred of humanity was still trying to hang out for five more minutes in the pool.

"But Mom, just five more minutes!"

"Okay, son."

I have to do something. This energy is consuming me, and I don't know how to get rid of it. It's not like I can grab any female off the street and have my way with her. Society has rules against that. But it has been so long since I've met someone I really care about—or at least give a damn enough to take home.

Yet *maybe . . . maybe she feels something, too?*

But that would be quite the long shot. Technically, we've only met once. But in that short conversation, she had held my gaze, she only looked away because she was shy. Alluring.

As I stare at myself in the mirror, I notice that the transformation hasn't undone the beginnings of the crow's feet around my eyes. Disappointing, but that's okay. At least the aging won't be going any further.

I had hoped turning into a distractor would have taken care of these oddities, but of course, it didn't; in fact, the transformation only seemed to make things worse, especially in regards to my personality.

My heart is still weak, and at the mercy of a human female.

According to the higher-ups, these feelings will remain forever. Unless, of course, I am somehow killed. Which, given the way they explained things, would not be an easy task.

At least I don't have to deal with the aging process again. This is so freeing in a way I can't explain. Getting old is such a cruel, earthly thing.

I've always thought the act of living itself plays out rather backward. My thinking is that everyone should be born old, with all that glorious wisdom—provided senility doesn't hit—and as time goes on, they will get younger as a sort of a reward. Then the whole process will stop in their twenties. Twenty-six years old—the best year, really. The time when a person is at their optimum, both physically and mentally.

Life shouldn't be the other way around. But then again, everything around here is backwards.

My wayward thoughts again drift to her. *I wonder what's she's doing right now. Probably burning her toast.* I curse at myself, wondering how I let such a frivolous creature capture the dark recesses of my heart.

If the mere thought of her can bring me so much happiness, what would it be like if we were actually together? What if these feelings never leave? Am I doomed for all eternity? Because let's face it, I've got loads of time.

Maybe meditating will help; I feel like my life could use some balance. Because I feel crooked as hell. But if I can't get her to love me the old-fashioned way, I suppose there are other ways of doing it.

I need to make a special trip to that windmill. The windmill will have the answers, it will know how to fix me.

THE BUS DRIVER

Bruce Reamer

*B*ruce could never stomach Sunday afternoons. The vile monster that is Monday always looms over him like a wet blanket. For him, the day can never be fully enjoyed, it's just a slow kind of hell. A delayed hiccup until a new crap storm of a week begins.

He lied his way through the entire interview and soon found his way into another job that he couldn't stand: driving another school bus. But starving isn't a viable option, and neither is being homeless, so he continues on with the job he hates. At least he knows how to do it.

He couldn't believe they hired him after the debacle last year when he drove his bus up a snowbank. He admits that, even for him, that was a little over the top, but he learned his lesson, he won't be doing that again.

Life wasn't always this miserable. There was a time back in high school that Bruce actually enjoyed himself—in welding class—but that was temporary, just six weeks. Other than that, his life has been pretty lackluster.

Drinking is the one thing that Bruce looks forward to—and let's face it, alcohol just makes life more fun. As soon as he gets home from work, he gets his favorite glass, crams it full of ice, and pours on the magic. Whiskey being his drink of choice.

He never liked his drinks neat, and didn't understand people who do. Maybe they feel the ice waters down the booze, but he would never give ice time to do that. He likes the way it clinks against the glass, his calling card to happiness.

While some drunks turn into different people entirely—mean SOBs or sobbing piles of garbage, for example—that just isn't his style. Bruce actually feels *empowered* when he drinks. He sees things and people for how they really are. His anger doesn't boil as hot after a shot. The sting of loneliness isn't so bad either. Drinking to him is a lifelong friend, so his top priority is to never run out of it.

Every single day at his job, he feels like a hamster on a wheel—running but getting nowhere in particular. Some days, he just longs for it to be over.

His employers will never know how close he's come to crashing his bus into a tree. Because lately, if he's forced to drive this bus much longer, he feels like he's one step away from doing just that. It's just a matter of time before he either blows his brains out, or crashes his bus into a pole.

A typical day goes like this: By the time the last rug rat steps off the bus, Bruce's migraine is firing on all cylinders—thankfully, drinking helps this. Buses are loud, and he would have thought by now he'd be used to it, but he can never get used to that kind of chaos. He just pretends he is.

He wants whiskey so bad now he can almost taste it. He closes his eyes and pictures how sweet it will be to taste it on his lips.

He can feel sweat forming on his brow, and the shakes are coming in strong now. He needs whiskey in the worst way, so when he spies Pony Road off in the distance, he decides that maybe he can find what he needs at Margie's bar.

Bruce has always felt like an outsider here. The elusive outlier, the awkward pause, the inappropriate-for-the-occasion dresser—these are all good descriptions of Bruce.

He's always felt like the bent part of a puzzle piece, and never did well with being made fun of. No one really does, but this hurt he carries from childhood, and it gnaws on him like a dog chewing a bone. Sometimes his anger rears its ugly head at times when it shouldn't. And it's no fun trying to act normal when you feel like a lit stick of dynamite.

And he knows the very day it happened. He was in the fourth grade, and his teacher was Ms. Murkle.

Ms. Murkle was not much of a looker. She always wore a stiff upper lip that was adorned with a faint mustache. Whenever he got close enough, he always wished he had a razor to shave that thing off. He didn't know how a lady could go through life looking like that.

Her eyeglasses were bent on one side and smeared to the point that they should have had their own windshield wipers. Each day, she wore a set of pearls and a dress in different colors that fit her like a gunnysack, only emphasizing the fact that she probably hadn't gotten lucky in a good decade. Not that Bruce would've made that connection back then.

She always loved to blow her nose, and when she did, she would shove used Kleenex up her sleeve like a squirrel hiding acorns. The other kids didn't seem to notice much, but he did.

And she never bothered Bruce until that fateful day in October.

During recess one afternoon, Bruce forgot to go to the bathroom because he was having too much fun on the monkey bars, and didn't hear the bell. As a child, he had a tendency to get lost in his own world, preferring the imaginary to reality. He had just enough time to hang up his coat and run into class.

Ms. Murkle had gone straight into the lesson that day, and he ran right to his desk. He didn't bother going to the bathroom, but that's what he should have done.

He knew as soon as he sat down that he had made the wrong choice. He had to pee so badly his leg wouldn't stop shaking.

He would just have to hold it.

He knew Ms. Murkle's track record when it came to boys and bathrooms: She tended to say no. She favored the girls, no matter what it was.

Barbara, the girl that sat in front of him, turned around, glancing down at his shaking leg. She saw his obvious discomfort, and seemed to sense what was wrong.

"Just tell her you have to go."

"You know she's gonna say no," he whispered back.

"Ask her anyway."

Barbara had always been sweet as pie to Bruce, and he had always liked her.

But if he didn't ask Ms. Murkle soon, he knew there would be an accident on the floor. He nodded at Barbara, thinking maybe it wouldn't hurt to ask. Reluctantly, he got up and shuffled to her desk.

Bracing himself for the answer he knew he was going to get, he stood beside her, waiting for her to look up from her book.

He knew she could see him standing there, but she wouldn't look up.

I guess this was a game she wanted to play.

I'll just stand here like some random idiot, because you're in complete control of how I hold my bladder. No problem.

"Ms. Murkle?"

"Yes."

Still not looking up from her book.

"Can I, um, go to the bathroom?"

Most of her face was hidden by her book, and apparently there was no need for her to look up from it. He was too unimportant.

"No, Bruce, you may not. Please sit down, and tend to your work."

What is the harm in letting me go to the bathroom?

This was the answer he was expecting, and arguing was only going to make her mad.

He walked back to his seat, past Barbara.

"Told you that witch wouldn't let me."

Her face fell. "I'm sorry. Just get up and go anyway."

"And be suspended? No, thanks."

He tried holding out a bit more, but it was no use. Nature took over, he just couldn't hold it anymore. Soon after, he felt wetness trickle down his leg.

He knew Barbara could hear him relieving himself, and he wanted to die. He stared down at the floor where an impressive pool was already forming at his feet. And for some reason, he felt the need to make up a song. Anything to take his mind off what was going on.

It is what it is as it trickles on down. It is what it is as my pee runs down. I'll make a mess on the floor like an animal, because you get off on humiliation, you hairy-faced bitch. Your privates probably got spiderwebs in it.

The puddle of urine was already trailing its way toward Stanley's foot. Of course it had to be Stanley sitting next to him, he was only the class bully.

It didn't matter what Stanley did; he would always come out smelling like a rose. Bruce knew his parents were important people at the school, so he supposed that explained things.

He held his breath as he could start to hear the students around him whispering. There was even a shriek from one of the girls.

Exaggerate much?

It didn't take long for Stanley to catch wind of it, and soon his screeching laugh joined in with the other yelling.

Good God, this can't get any worse.

Bruce was ready for it; he felt it coming. He was the court jester in a one-act play, dancing around like the village idiot. He had put his armor on, puffed up his chest, and set his jaw—it was okay. If this was what life was going to throw at him, then, go ahead, throw the biggest banana cream pie you can find.

Except, nothing about this was ok.

A few other people joined in on the laughter, but not everyone. Some lowered their heads in shame as if they were the ones that whizzed in their pants.

Well, at least there were a couple students with a heart at that godforsaken school.

He didn't know what to do next. He supposed he could just sit there in his soggy pants, all red-faced and mortified. When Ms. Murkle finally figured out what happened—which took entirely too long--she just stared out into space like she didn't have two brain cells to rub together.

Heck of a time to fall ignorant.

He hated her so much in that moment that he wanted to bash her head into that damn desk of hers. He watched as she quick ran to the shelf to grab a roll of paper towels. God, this whole scene was pathetic. He did notice her half-hearted attempt at cleaning it up, wiping it in repeated circles with the bottom of her heel before she ran out of the room.

Like wiping it over and over again was going to make all this go away.

He was still sitting in his chair, facing the cacophony of laughter from his classmates.

Barbara glanced at him, tears in her eyes. He could feel a surge of hurt and humiliation rising up in him, taking away his peace, and self-worth.

He got up and ran out of the classroom, down the street and the full two miles back home. He didn't bother with his coat or homework, he didn't even look back.

And since that day, he never felt *well* again.

MARGIE SUTTON

Margie Sutton

Margie woke up not feeling like herself. This isn't all that unusual; she's felt this way before—maybe a few times, in fact.

She willed herself to get out of bed despite the depleted feeling from the night before. Hearing the birds sing outside her window, was a comfort. And the morning light was hitting the portion of her bar in such a way that made it easy to get up, too. She could hear Adam and Eve scrambling around downstairs.

They need to get outside.

Today is going to call for a Bloody Mary; she can feel it in her bones. She gravitates toward the fridge, pleased to find a few stalks of leftover celery. She washes them off, pulling at the pesky strings and cutting them at an angle so they can fit pretty in her glass. She grabs the tray of green olives left over from the night before.

Maybe she's becoming a little hoity-toity in her old age.

As much as she doesn't want it, she's going to insist on a meeting. Things have to be decided, important things. And she will need the power of her sister, as much as she wants to resist it.

Problem is, she loathes dealing with her. Mavis is duplicitous, and not to mention, horribly unpredictable. She's also the queen of outbursts. Margie would never know what sort of thing might set her off. But in the same vein, she's also a force to be reckoned with, and let's face it, she is powerful. She knows all about the powers that were freely given to her, even if Margie doesn't understand it.

In simple terms, one could categorize her sister as a sort of a witch. Margie doesn't know what Mavis is really—maybe she's the first of her kind. But Margie prefers to stay far, far away from anything that even hints at hocus-pocus.

Mavis just plain scares her.

Margie can recall a time that her twin wasn't so powerful. In her formative years, her sister's mind had been so cluttered with hormones or a chemical imbalance—whatever it was—that she could barely walk straight.

She had been perfectly normal until the sixth grade. Margie and her sister were fraternal twins, and they couldn't be any more different in personalities and looks, but they enjoyed life. They both played soccer, spent time with friends, and liked horses.

Mavis had been a good student. Margie remembers her laughing and kicking the ball with her in the bright sunshine. All those days of playing soccer, their futures bright and promising, happy memories that she will always cherish.

Somewhere though, between the sixth and seventh grade, something had shifted inside of Mavis. It was like an invisible storm cloud had moved in, raining down on everything that had once made her happy.

Margie kept hoping the dark cloud would just leave, but it wouldn't. And no one had seen it coming—it came out of the blue and stayed—and no one knew how to deal with it.

Mavis's decline happened over the span of a year. Things that had once been easy now were a chore. Things that had once made her happy, like horses and taking pictures, now caused her frustration and worry. She didn't even like touching her horse statues—in fact, she became afraid of them, thinking they were covered in germs.

Mavis put all her horse statues away in her closet—she'd told Margie she didn't want them staring at her. Nearly every night, she would wake up screaming, saying the horses were talking to her from the closet and telling her worrisome things. Mom finally had to get rid of them.

With each month, she grew more isolated and moody, preferring to spend all of her time in her room rather than with family. But because these things could have easily been explained away—growing pains or just teenage malaise—and that's what her parents first thought, no one thought too much about it.

But then she started coming up with rather elaborate and incessant demands. She would only eat certain kinds of foods and in specific combinations. She didn't like to eat with family—she preferred eating by herself, on her own terms. She would often get up in the middle of the night—waking Margie and everyone else up while making her own strange concoctions. And it wasn't all that different than the meal that was made at dinner. Margie could always hear her running the microwave in the middle of the night.

When she was done with her midnight snack, she would trudge back down the hallway, slamming the door to her room. She always left a trail of garbage wherever she went. She never would pick it up, she thought it was covered in germs.

In the morning, every cupboard door and every light in the house was turned on. Like a devious fairy had come flying in through the window, waving her wand of chaos.

Mavis could go through a roll of paper towels in one evening. But could she use a kitchen towel?

No.

Kitchen towels were filthy and filled with germs.

Even when freshly laundered and out of the dryer.

Since Margie's room was in the basement, she could often hear Mavis roaming the halls. Back and forth she would go, her hard footfalls sounding like a Sasquatch as she wore lines into the living room carpet. And meanwhile, the microwave would be beeping because she was busy in the bathroom. With Mavis, everything was on her timing, and everything was done with vigor.

And don't get her started on water. She would often get glasses of it throughout the night--and use a different glass each time.

In the morning they would all be lined up like bowling pins ready to be scored.

It's a wonder their parents didn't lose their ever-loving minds.

Their father had worked long hours at a plant, so he wasn't privy to all the frightful scenarios Mavis would often invent. Mom had taken the brunt of Mavis's storm, and her near-constant discord had taken its toll.

Their wonderful mom, who, in the early days, was easy with a smile and usually in good spirits, was now a shadow of her formal self. Her eyes lacked the sparkle they once had, and daily living had become difficult.

Margie felt very guilty about this, and every night she would pray that she wouldn't wake up with brains like that. She was terrified that maybe the craziness would start seeping into her.

As Mavis's twin, she often wondered if going insane was unavoidable, like getting your period or catching the common cold.

She expected any day for the crazy to start rearing its ugly head. Sometimes she would wake up in the middle of the night, and do a running check of herself.

Am I still normal?

Yes.

Do I hear voices?

No.

She often thought that the crazy might latch onto her while she was sleeping, like it was some tangible thing you could inhale while you slept.

The few times their parents did try standing up to Mavis, it would never end well. The first time was when they'd just finished grocery shopping and were all walking out to their car. Mavis was agitated and screaming about not getting a certain thing, and it was a struggle just walking with her in the parking lot.

She was embarrassing.

The hard part was that Mavis never seemed aware of her own behavior. Margie often thought of her twin as a feral animal, and being forced to ride in a car with a crazy person is one of the cruelest things anyone should ever have to endure. Many times she wished she could just open the door and jump the hell out of it.

At one point, Mom was just tired of the screaming, so she dropped her off on the side of the road. Mavis climbed out. Margie remembers seeing Mavis jumping up and down like she was on fire through the rear window. To anyone that drove past, they probably thought her to be a raging lunatic.

It didn't take very long for mom to lose her nerve, and turn that car back around.

So much for a peaceful afternoon.

When they came back, Mavis was sitting there on the curb, all wide-eyed and dirty, in almost a catatonic like state. Margie could never figure out how she managed to get so completely covered in dirt from head to toe-it's not like mom was gone for that long. Margie pictured her, in those four short minutes, rolling around in someone's yard like a dog. The residents of the nearby houses probably got a good chuckle out of that one.

The crazy was in her eyes, and Margie hated her for it. The last thing she wanted was for her sister to get back into that car. But alas, she was family, and they were twins. There was nowhere else for her to go.

After that episode, Mavis spent the next two weeks in bed.

School soon became impossible for both their parents and Mavis. So she stopped going altogether. Peers were often cruel, and the teachers and counselors were starting to lose their patience.

No one could figure out what was wrong with her, and they were starting to give up. Margie couldn't blame them, Mavis could test the saints.

Several mornings, she'd seen her mom at the stove, making scrambled eggs. She made the best scrambled eggs ever, even when she was tired. Margie would often watch her, standing there half-asleep by the pan, scrambling the eggs with a spatula as tears cascaded down her face. She'd watched as one rolled down her cheek and fell into the pan. Margie didn't mind; in fact, she hadn't said a word. She knew exactly why her mom had been crying.

She was a good mom, and nothing could change that. Sometimes Margie wished her sister would get admitted to a mental facility. But that required money that her family didn't have. And besides, her mom wouldn't have the heart to do it anyway.

Comments from others were cruel. People often said Mavis was their parents' fault, that something horrible must have happened to her for her to act this way. *Things like that just don't happen, kids aren't born that way.*

Truth of the matter is, some kids *are* just born that way. Their parents had given in to Mavis's every possible whim.

And it still wasn't good enough.

No matter what medications they gave Margie's sister, however easy they made things for her to land, Mavis was mentally ill. And the family would always be under a microscope.

It was a sad realization.

Margie takes another sip of her Bloody Mary, savoring the taste, remembering how good they can be.

It has been entirely too long since I had one of these.

She's delaying the inevitable; she knows that. But she's going to have to call Mavis, no matter how much she doesn't want to. The group at the bar last night thought it best she do the contacting. But with these distractor things running around, things were getting way out of hand, and something had to be done.

Mavis was out-of-her-mind nuts, but she was a force to be reckoned with. Margie eyed the telephone, half-hoping that when she picked up, she wouldn't hear a dial tone.

She knew Mavis would know she was trying to call her as soon as she dialed the numbers. The most irritating part about being her twin was that she couldn't run away from her thoughts.

Mavis would always hear them.

She pours herself another drink, her procrastination game strong.

She will call Mavis, her twin, *the karmic.* Of all the people in this town, she will know what to do.

THE PRICK

Brooke

I knew it was him right away—he was wearing cutoff jean shorts and a wifebeater. And if hair could talk, his screamed in all caps: NUTSO. It was bleached out and fried, poking out of his head like some scarecrow guarding a hayfield.

Lance, aka "The Prick," was down at the edge of the lake with beer in hand, chatting up poor Lyle. And Lyle has the patience of a saint—he's married to Cassie, after all—and being the nice man that he is, probably giving The Prick a rundown of all the prime fishing holes in the area.

Cassie's standing next to me on her porch. One hand on her hip, the other occupied with a drink. I can smell vodka on her breath, and I wonder what she thinks about this little impromptu visit. I watch as she stares long and hard at Scout's possible stepfather.

"You know, my sister can sure pick 'em," she says.

She sips from her drink, stirring the rest of it with her finger. She's taken full inventory of the Prick, and I can only imagine what she thinks of him.

With more effort than required, we all—Scout and Lyle included—watch as The Prick tries making his way up the steep hill to Cassie's cabin. They have steps, but for whatever reason, he chooses not to use them, which only makes him look more ridiculous. He appears to be both drunk and high, if one can surmise the difference.

I'm trying hard not to laugh at him out loud, because after watching him, that's exactly what you'd want to do.

After he finally arrives on top, he stumbles his way over to us. His shorts had fallen down to his knees, revealing his underwear. He quick pulls them up, hoping to cover up his gaffe. He looks around, glances over at the lawn and scowls. "Someone needs to mow this goddamn grass."

Sure, blame the grass.

"Lyle takes care of it just fine," Cassie retorts.

She eyes the Prick like one would an insect. She doesn't openly show her affection for Lyle, but if the occasion calls for it, she can lambaste his critics like a punch in the face.

"We all took bets on whether you were gonna make it up here or not," she says.

"Well, I'm happy for ya." He responds.

He reeks of BO, and I'm immediately reminded of our school bus.

And I'm beginning to see why Scout is glad to be out of Florida.

He leans in towards me, and I have to take a step back. "Nice to meet you, young lady."

"Thanks."

Scout rolls her eyes. "Where's Mom?"

"Probably getting her ass bit up by mosquitos. Christ—they ought to be your state bird." He glares at me as if I am in charge of all the biting insects.

"They're pretty prevalent this year," I concede before adding, "I hope you brought some bug spray."

"Well, I hope she did, too, because I don't pack."

I bet you don't do a lot of things.

Scout doesn't look too happy. Her mom and The Prick had come into town only hours before, and this visit seems to make her uncomfortable. I watch as she picks at her face, a nervous habit she's been doing more frequently.

Scout's mom, *Linda,* comes walking up. She's tall and grand, and I'm struck by how strange it is for her to be paired with the Prick.

They are about as mismatched as anyone can be, but then again, the journey of life can create strange pairings. I don't know if I'll ever truly understand how two people can get together. She comes in with a warm smile.

"Hello, there! Cassie has told me so much about you. How lucky she is to have found a friend here in—what's the name of this town again?"

Scout gives her a funny look.

"Really, Mom? Aunt Cassie's only lived here for the last ten years; how can you not remember the name of it?"

"Oh, I know the name of the town Scout, I was just being silly."

I watch as a giant mosquito lands on her cheek. She slaps it away, leaving a fresh smear of blood across her face.

"Oh, these things are driving me nuts. I have welts around my ankles already—can you believe that?"

"They do get bad this time of year," I offer. "They'll die down when it gets cooler."

I don't have the heart to tell her that they'll probably be hanging out for the rest of the summer. I am either immune to them, or they have tasted enough of my own blood to be uninterested.

"Well, bugs or not, it beats the weather down in Florida," her mom replies. "Right now, it's so hot down there I can barely breathe. It's nice not having to sweat out of my clothes every fifteen minutes. Even if I do risk getting eaten alive."

The Prick pipes up. "Well, we best be getting into different clothes if we're going on a boat."

Ah, right. The boat ride.

Good lord I hope he takes a shower first.

I watch as Linda scrunches up her face. "Yes, how sweet! A pontoon boat."

Scout leans in and whispers in my ear. "She acts like she owns a catamaran."

The Prick keeps going. "I need to jump in the shower quick—I wouldn't want you all jumpin' off the boat because of my stink."

Wise choice.

"Yes, please do." Cassie nods, waving him away. Her face pinches as she takes another sip of her drink. She must have caught a whiff of him, too.

I stare as the two of them walk back to Cassie and Lyle's cabin. Cassie lingers still, admiring some of the flowers at her doorstep. Lyle snorts behind his glass from where he's sitting off to the side, silently observing.

Scout moves in closer, lowering her voice so only I can hear. "I found out about this an hour before they got here." She rolls her eyes.

"Aren't you glad to see your mom?"

"Yeah, but why does he have to tag along? It's like he has something on her. And God, he stinks like holy hell."

"They do seem mismatched."

"I know, right?" She sighs.

"I'll come on the boat with you if you need me," I offer, hoping I don't regret it later.

Her eyes light up. "Really! I don't think I can sit there by myself just watching them play all kissy face. By the way, did you notice how drunk he was?"

I give a half-shrug. "Kinda hard to miss."

"And what the hell was it with those stairs? I mean, my God, he's a clown."

I couldn't help but laugh.

"Maybe I can stay at your house tonight?"

"Scout, don't you want to catch up with your mom? I mean, that's why they're here."

"Really? Are you kidding me right now? Brooke, the only reason they're here is because my mom can't stand being down in Florida right now, she hates the heat."

My face falls. "I'm sorry."

"And he always smells like a trash bin. It's embarrassing!"

As Scout launches into another story about The Prick, I see the outline of someone in the distance. I recognize him right away—Marcus—and I have never been so glad to see someone in my whole life.

Of course, Cassie notices him, too. I can tell by the way he's walking that he has something important to say, but before he can, Cassie interjects herself, like she always does.

"And who is your friend, dear?" She says this with the biggest smile on her face.

Good lord women, give him time to walk up.

"This is Marcus."

Cassie flashes him an exuberant smile, and Lyle rolls his eyes. She had smiled like that when she met Aaron, too.

Oh, Aaron.

Cassie gets right up in his face. "Say, are you doing anything? Because you should come with us on the boat."

"A boat? Um, sure? I guess." Marcus blinks before strengthening his stance. "Sure, but I do have someone else with me."

"Well, of course, the more, the merrier. But where is this person?" she asks, scanning the yard. Is he hiding?"

"No ma'am. He'll be coming; he's just a slow walker."

I scan the yard, too, hoping to see who Marcus is talking about.

"Well, that settles it then. We'll be leaving shortly." Cassie winks at him then walks away, Lyle trailing behind her.

I wait until she's out of earshot. "What is going on, Marcus?"

"There's a good chance some of your friends here are distractors. I need to get on that boat."

Marcus eyes The Prick walking out of the house, his hair still wet. That was a quick shower.

"Who is that?"

"You don't want to know, trust me. But it could be Scout's soon-to-be stepdad."

"Okay, well, I brought a friend of my own. He's going to be help-ing us."

"With what? Killing distractors?"

He leans in. "We'll talk about this later, Brooke. And please, be a heck of a lot more discreet about it. You don't have to worry; I'm not going to let anything happen on that boat. Not during daylight anyway."

DEMON BIRDS

Brooke

The air is heavy. We're in that time of the afternoon where things drag at a snail's pace, and the mosquitos won't leave us alone, gorging on our skin every two seconds.

Marcus talked his way onto the boat, but that didn't take much effort since he'd caught Cassie's eye. If a person is male and even *moderately* attractive, Cassie will make sure she crosses their path—and then she'll hit on them.

She has a way about her that makes a person feel special, even if they happen to be the biggest square peg in the box of life. She loves nothing more than flirting with members of the opposite sex, especially hot-blooded ones that drip with masculinity. And Marcus fits the bill perfectly.

I wonder how she would feel if she knew that Marcus had dealt Ethel's fatal blow. Like me, he had found himself in an impossible situation.

Ethel's demise was unnatural, so this secret will have to stay ours, even if it feels like a betrayal. We will have to keep lots of things under wraps until we figure out how to defeat these distractors.

I am intrigued by the "friend" tagging along with Marcus on Lyle's boat, and I can't help but stare at him. His whole demeanor screams supernatural of some sort. I want to ask him outright, but it feels rude. And anyway, hadn't Marcus told me to keep these things quiet?

I don't know why he's here, and it's bugging me. Though, if Marcus brought him, he must have a sound reason.

Marcus seems to revel in keeping me out of the loop.

We all make our way onto the boat. I find a seat next to him, and lean in, whispering.

"Why don't you ever tell me what's going on around here? It's annoying. Like, why are you on this boat, and who is your friend?"

Marcus just sits there, brooding as he nurses his beer. "Actually, Brooke, I think it's better if you're on a 'need to know' basis."

I almost punch him right in the face. "Really, Marcus?"

His companion snorts, and I wait for the introductions. *Lucky me.*

Marcus leans over, whispering in my ear. "I don't trust anyone here. And believe me, you and what's in your best interest are my top priorities, remember that."

"Really? I guess I need reminding sometimes," I snipe back.

What a standard pat-ass answer.

"So, um, Traveller, this is Brooke Larkin. Her parents own the resort down the way."

I watch as this *Traveller* looks over at me, his eyes piercing. I wait for him to look away, but he doesn't.

How rude. And how pretentious do you have to be to call yourself 'The Traveller'?

The last thing I need is another supernatural with the ego of King Kong.

"The name was bestowed on me, Miss. I didn't acquire it myself."

Since I didn't utter that last statement out loud, I cringe.

Great, someone else who can read my mind. Just what I need.

He looks straight at me, saying out loud, "Yes, I did."

What an arrogant ass. Why can't I just hang around regular people? And what is it about supernaturals and their freaky-looking eyes?

"Nice to meet you," I manage.

Marcus glances over at me. "His wife stayed home. She doesn't care for the mosquitos."

"I don't blame her." I turn to the newcomer. "Who's your wife?"

"Penny."

I knew this Penny! It was coming back to me now. Her family had stayed at our resort several times over the years. And I had seen him on occasion. He always seemed rather aloof, like he was in the presence of people that were *beneath* him.

Scout studies him. I'm grateful to have her here. I can see her trying to piece the disjointed parts of the conversation in her mind, and I wonder what she's thinking.

I glance up to see the Traveller's attention turn toward the Prick. He and Marcus are both staring at him, their heads cocked and brows furrowed.

"Who is that peculiar-looking man?" the Traveller asks.

Oh, this is about to get good.

Marcus glares at him. "It would appear that every village has an idiot."

I can hear bits and pieces of a story the Prick is telling about some fight he was once involved in. His gestures are animated, making it seem like it had occurred moments ago.

"The dude was casing me out, man; I had to defend myself."

"What are you talking about, Lance?" Scout's mom, like everyone else, has been listening to every painful word coming out of his mouth. But not because his story's interesting; more on the lines of—crazy-ass train wreck that you can't stop watching. Lunatics always garner full attention, I suppose.

I wonder what Scout's mom possibly sees in him. He doesn't appear to have a lick of sense-but then again, maybe she doesn't either.

Marcus jumps in. "So, you're a fighter?"

The Prick looks him over with a grin. "Yes, sir."

"And what transpired from there?"

"Transpired?"

The Prick stares blankly for a few moments before shaking his head as if to clear it. "It's like the can of corn was talking itself right off the shelf, begging me to whip it at the guy. It couldn't be helped, you know?"

"I'm sure it couldn't. And where did this confrontation take place?"

Scout's mom piped up. "Gas station."

Cassie takes a long puff of her cigarette before she starts laughing.

"So, the plot thickens," says the Traveller.

"My aim wasn't too great, but he got me good, right between eyes. After that, it was lights out." He points at the middle of his forehead. "I had a goose egg for weeks."

"That explains a lot." Cassie says while nursing her drink. Lyle grins but keeps his eye on the boat.

"I'm kinda proud of it."

"I bet you are," Marcus mutters under his breath.

I watch as The Prick continues on with his colorful version of events. Marcus and the Traveller are hanging on every word she says. The Prick is like the rogue dinner guest about to yank at the edge of the tablecloth, sending everything to the floor.

Lyle however, is completely uninterested in the Prick's tales, and appears to be lost in thought. This isn't anything new, he always keeps to himself, and I wonder if that ever bothers Cassie, since she's quite the opposite. I know if I was married to him, it would drive me insane.

I have to find a way for Lyle to open up to me.

The lake is busy tonight with the near-constant croaking of frogs and fish heads surfacing every few minutes. Everything is alive, hungry, and biting. The bug spray isn't doing much good,—in fact, it seems to be encouraging them.

"Are any of those things on the boat with us?" I whisper to Marcus.

"You need to be more discrete about asking," he hisses back. "If they were, they would have heard your every word. But no, there are no distractors here."

"Good to know." Getting info out of Marcus is like pulling teeth. He's the annoying older brother I never had—and never wanted.

"Although, for him," he points at the Prick, "it would be a most definite improvement."

I snicker quietly as Lyle perks up. "Everyone get your binoculars ready! The nest is up ahead."

Neelsville is the home of the famed eagle's nest, and it sits high in the branches of the tallest tree, right before Carver Island. The locals here are pretty proud of it.

Lyle navigates the boat around a few known stumps as the familiar outline of pines comes into view. He turns off the boat motor and grabs his binoculars, adjusting them as he stares into the forest. "Hmm. The mama doesn't seem to be around."

Almost everyone on the boat is looking at the nest now, and Cassie's the only one without binoculars. If it doesn't involve men or alcohol, she's pretty vacant.

Things around us have turned silent. As the boat trolls downstream amongst the reeds, I notice that the Traveller's eyes are scanning our surroundings, darting back and forth just a little too quickly. His lips tighten into a grim line, and he whispers something to Marcus. I wish I could have heard him, but I catch part of it.

". . . ready for whatever."

Ready for what? I think.

I feel Marcus's hot breath at my ear. "Whatever happens, stay close and don't move. I'll protect you."

"Protect me from what? What's going on?"

Of course, he doesn't answer, and I motion for Scout to sit close, and thank God, she doesn't question it. But her eyes start darting around, too.

"What's going on?" she asks.

"I'm in the dark as always," I quip, "but something's about to go down. I'm sure we'll find out soon enough."

I search the sky. I hate this, because if this Traveller guy is rattled, we may be in for some trouble.

"There's something in the nest!" Lyle yelled.

I see something dark moving in the nest, but without binoculars, I can't tell what it is.

Lyle calls out. "No!!"

"What's going on?" I ask.

"A predator's attacking the nest!"

My stomach drops. "Oh no, they're just babies! Where's the momma?"

"Probably looking for food," Lyle suggests.

We all stare as a dark, winged creature comes into full view, flying right in the direction of our boat. I'm amazed at its size.

"Start yelling!" Lyle calls.

We all scream, but it doesn't help. Soon after, a cluster of birds are swarming our boat, and circling above us like they are on an invisible merry-go-around.

"These birds are aggressive!" Lyle yells, swatting at one that's trying to peck at his head.

"Take cover!" Marcus screams.

Take cover? Where do you take cover on a boat?

At that moment, I feel the weight of him on top of me as he bends over Scout and I, his strong arms clutching us. They are heavy and muscular, and I am overcome with gratitude.

Thank God you're here.

I can see from underneath his arm that one of the birds is attacking Cassie. It's poking at her hair in mean little pecks, the air soon fills with her screams.

"Get away from me!!" she shouts, flapping her arms as she shoos it away.

"Oh my word!!" Scout shrieks, clearly seeing the same thing I am.

Black birds are everywhere. The sky isn't blue anymore—they have all blocked out the sun.

Another bird grabs ahold of Cassie's arm, nipping at it, and trails of blood start running down her skin and dripping into the boat's deck. It feels wrong just sitting there underneath Marcus's arm, but he had us in a tight hold, and he isn't budging.

He whispers in my ear. "Stay still, Brooke."

All the commotion has sobered up The Prick, and he's openly fighting them with both hands. I watch as his beer dances precariously on the rail of the boat. He grabs at a bird that took a swipe at his collar and catches it midair, squeezing its neck. Impressive, considering he is half-bombed. I immediately feel guilty about my initial impression of him.

The dying bird falls to the floor of the boat with a thud. The feathers on it are shiny, and the beak is overly pronounced and curved. Its eyes, still open, have a purplish hue. It looks like one of those fake plastic crows one might find at a hobby store.

"Don't look at them!" Marcus shouts.

He is reading my mind, but I don't care; I want them gone. They are surrounding the boat now, banging into the sides, into people—and making cackling noises while doing it. A couple of them are biting the boat like it's a snack.

They are enjoying this.

Another bird takes a stab at Linda's arm, and her shrieks join Cassie's. She tries slapping it off, but it keeps coming back for more. I can feel Marcus's anger; he wants to help them, but he doesn't want to take his arms off me or Scout.

I can see part of the Traveller—he's sitting there, staring. As if he's communicating with the birds in some way, all this chaos does not appear to be affecting him. In fact, one of them lands on his shoulder, and I catch him talking to it.

"For these purposes, you need to."

Everything stops. Nothing moves. The boat, the wind, the chirpings of nature—even the people seem afraid to breathe. And when I do, I'm surprised I still can.

A mist is circling above us now, surrounding the boat, a nebulous gray cloud swirling about each soul on board. Everything around me feels slow, like it's suddenly hard to take in information. I feel like I just breathed in laughing gas. I giggle out loud at how quickly this has affected me. I'm feeling both euphoric and clueless, and for a moment, it feels delightful, despite the circumstances.

What is causing this?

As the smoke dissipates, I see an appearance of a man sitting next to the Traveller, and the first thing I notice is his shoes: they're a black patent leather—out of place given the casualness of the boat. He has an ease with the Traveller that only two people that know each other could have, but the Traveller's glare is frosty. And a little disgusted.

I can't bring myself to acknowledge whoever this is, and I'm afraid to look in his direction. There's just something so negative about him that I don't want to acknowledge.

I can feel his dark energy. He *wants* me to look in his direction. I struggle to keep my gaze away.

Again, I feel him trying to worm his way into my head. A stabbing pain shoots behind my ears next and travels ever so slowly to the back of my neck. I recognize this pain—*this is the same feeling I had when Ethel tried getting into my head at the picnic.* I'd forgotten how excruciating this is, but the painful memory comes flooding back like an icy, poisonous gruel.

I try forcing it out, but just like with Ethel, it doesn't budge. And the longer it's there, the more intense it becomes. This feels stronger than what I encountered with Ethel. It's sharper, more aggressive.

And then I hear the words: *You will see me.*

He is trying to take over, trying to put me under some kind of spell, and I have no choice but to look his way.

I attempt a final appeal for my freedom.

I don't want to look at you.

Oh, but you will.

I feel myself giving way to it. Before I pass out, I catch him as he flicks off a mosquito with his razor-sharp claws. I tremble at the sight of it. It's so *unnatural.*

"LET HER BE!"

The Traveller yells these words so loud, it wakes me up a little, and I watch as he stares at the thing like one would an enemy. Marcus leaps upright to attack, but the Traveller puts his arm up, shaking his head.

I scrunch up my nose. The air smells foul, like a forgotten dead mouse in the sun.

The thing turns his attention to the Traveller. "Tell me, do you ever tire of it?"

"Of what?" the Traveller asks.

"This, right here, right now. Immersed in all this nature."

He doesn't answer, but the Traveller's annoyance is obvious.

"God's country, I tell you."

"And what do you know of God?"

The thing's sinister laugh is so loud that the harsh echo bounces across the lake, scattering the nearby birds back into the trees.

Only the ones with the odd-looking feathers remain. I can see them gathered in groups of twos along the railing of the boat. They are watching and listening, and I have no doubt they understand everything being said.

"Well, my friend, he sure knows about you."

The Traveller sighs. "Well, that's good to know, Avalone; tell him I said hi."

Avalone sneers. "I have no interest in talking with him."

"I know, you don't. So, humor me; why are you here?"

"Aren't you pleased to see me?" The thing chuckles. "It's been a good while."

"Not long enough." The Traveller narrows his eyes at the intruder.

"Oh, Traveller, you've always had the worst of manners. Haven't you learned by now the proper way to treat your friends?"

"We both know we're not here to talk about my manners, Avalone. Go tell your flying bats to be on their merry way."

The glare the thing gives the Traveller is the stuff of nightmares.

"My flying bats, as you call them, happen to be starving right at this very moment. Did you know that? And this nice lot of humans here would make such a glorious dinner. Keep that in mind as you're talking with me."

I shudder at his words.

"What do you want, Avalone?" The Traveller's voice is low, dispassionate, and I wonder if he really cares about anything at all. "You've always had a stick up your ass, Traveller. You really ought to be more hospitable. All those thousands of years of living, and yet it has done nothing for your demeanor. By the way, you're looking a bit long in the tooth." The thing snickers at his own joke.

"I don't care what I look like, Avalone. Now tell your friends to leave. I mean it."

Avalone scans him head to toe and smiles. "No need for hostility. I didn't realize this occasion required an invite."

I can't help but stare at the frightful creature as they converse. His claws protrude out of his sleeves and appear to be at least half a foot long. And God, the eyes. I can't look directly at them for too long.

Avalone sighs dramatically when the Traveller doesn't reply. "After all we've been through together."

"Don't compare yourself to me. We have crossed paths, yes. But you will never be welcome here, Avalone. So why do you keep coming back?"

I notice then that everyone on the boat has stopped mid-motion. Some are sitting, a couple are still standing. All the humans anyway. The Prick has both hands still in the air. Everyone looks like inanimate dolls, stuck in various positions around the boat. Some are sitting, a couple are standing. Even Scout is in a trance. Marcus, the Traveller, and I are the only ones who seem to be able to move.

I wonder why I still can.

"Why has everyone stopped moving?" I whisper to the Traveller.

He just shakes his head no.

"Let's get down to the business of things, shall we?" The thing points at Marcus, whose icy glare is set to kill, his hand still gripping my arm and holding me just a little behind him.

"Your brooding, bulky friend over there has made a mess of things."

"How so?"

"He killed one of my prized pets. I had such plans for her, too. He ruined it with his short fuse. Unwise on his part."

I feel the heat coming off Marcus in waves, and my arm feels like it's on fire.

"You killed that innocent women, you and your henchmen," the Traveller argues.

Marcus growls. "Let the *Man Upstairs* sort it out. I don't have that kind of time."

The Traveller places his hand on Marcus's shoulder in warning.

"Avalone, take your flying misfits and head on back to wherever you came from."

"Misfits?" Avalone scoffs. "You should show me a little more respect, Traveller. I've done an abundance of things for you over the years, or have you forgotten?"

"I remember."

"Let's see, if memory serves, I recall you having a rather difficult time regarding the elements. What was is it again?" He chuckles. "Ah, yes, how could I possibly forget? It's the fire, isn't it? If I remember correctly, don't you spontaneously combust when you meddle too much in the lives of humans? *Please* tell me that ailment still doesn't have a hold of you?"

The Traveller doesn't answer.

The thing's laughter rings out over his thunderous applause. "After all these years? Good heavens, the Man upstairs does carry a grudge."

The Traveller's countenance is calm, but I sense Avalone is getting to him. "You should leave, Avalone. There's nothing for you here."

"Oh, I beg to differ. There's plenty here."

Before the conversation gets out of hand, I blurt out a question. "Why has everything stopped?"

The thing looks at me, and I immediately regret asking.

"Because I compelled them to, my dear. How interesting, though, that you appear unaffected." He turns to the Traveller. "I wonder why that is."

Scout is still in a trancelike state like everyone else. I try shaking her, but she doesn't respond. She has the same look that Patty had when Mom would catch her sleepwalking around the house.

It was unsettling to see everyone so still, and powerless.

The sound of the thing's voice renders me unable to move. He asks me a question. "Do you have relatives in the spiritual arts?"

I think of mom and how she knew about things. Thank God that ability skipped my sister—and that she isn't on this boat.

I glance over at him, tentatively. "No."

He looks over towards the Traveller. "Care to explain my abilities, Traveller, or should I? I know the fighter over there doesn't have a clue."

The Traveller clears his throat. "Avalone can change time, among other things. But believe me, he was just leaving."

"Well, that's a rather droll introduction. Good Lord; remind me not to use you as the town crier. You'd bore everyone to death over your coma-inducing commentary. Give it the fervor it deserves, Traveller. *I AM TO BE RECOGNIZED!"*

His booming voice makes the birds in the area start squawking from the trees. The creature snaps his clawed hand together, and the rest of them fly off into the distance. His eyes blaze red as he catches the Traveller with a piercing stare.

"You know what I want. I could eat every human being in this town—it would be so much fun for me. I'm especially intrigued by the girl." He smirks. "You know my feelings on the matter. Your fighter friend best stay out of my way."

"Where's Aaron?" I ask.

The thing laughs again. "Oh, we have such plans for him. He's safe and well in our care, and the next time you see him, he will, shall we say, be of a different sort."

I hate to think of what they are doing to Aaron. I grit my teeth, fighting to stay still when all I want to do is rip his red eyes out.

"I see time differently than you do, young lady. The elements are, shall we say, vast and manipulatable. I can feel time, too."

"And how would you *feel* time?" I query.

"Think of it as an envelope. It overlaps, recreates itself—I can rip it apart if I like. It's quite fun, especially when you get the hang of it. I would love to teach you everything I know, but alas, that's for another time. I do find your question rather endearing, though."

"You won't touch her!" Marcus screams, lurching forward.

"Oh, Marcus, do shut up!" Avalone barks back.

The Traveller's voice is unwavering, bold. "Enough, Avalone."

"You wouldn't want to catch on fire, friend." He laughs out loud.

"Coming from you, I can handle it."

Avalone stares long and hard at the Traveller. "Do you really want to see this beautiful boat and everything in it baked to a crisp? You're lucky I'm in a good mood. You can thank the girl for that."

Avalone's clawed hand reaches over and grazes my jawline, and at first I think he's going to break the skin. But he doesn't. He just stares into my eyes. I can't look away, no matter how badly I want to. His rich, bloody eyes mesmerize with both fear and anticipation.

"I'll be seeing you later. You can be quite sure about that."

He turns toward Marcus. "And I'd better not run into you."

The creature vanishes in an instant. Where he just sat is now an empty seat, covered in a cloud of vapor and smoke. It swirls around everyone, and as it does, people start waking up in shifts.

The Traveller leans in toward me.

"They won't know a thing. All they'll remember is the birds when they first started to attack. Please don't discuss what just happened."

"I won't."

I watch as one by one, everyone starts waking up from their Avalone-induced naps.

"Where's my drink?" Cassie says.

I roll my eyes. That would be her first reaction.

"Oh, look at my arms! Did something bite me? There's blood all over them!"

"It appears we ran into some very aggressive birds," the Traveller says. "They're all gone now."

I see Lyle come to the driver's side of the boat. He glances around, his face scrunched together like he doesn't know what's going on. Scout starts waking up, too, her eyes starting to show a little more life.

"What just happened?" she asks, turning toward me.

I don't know what to say to her, other than, "You don't want to know."

SCOUT

Brooke

I glance out the window just in time to see Scout stomping up to my house. She leans into our screen door, almost to the point of breaking. "Feel like coming over?"

There's an urgency to her voice and eyes, and I notice that her arms are covered in scratches.

"What happened to you?"

"Are you coming or not?"

I frown, shrugging. "Sure."

I grab a sweatshirt and follow her off the porch. Cassie's house isn't far, we're there in under a minute. I step into the kitchen just as she's making a beeline for Cassie's liquor cabinet.

"I could use a drink." She smiles. "Dumb bitch left everything unlocked."

Her statement about Cassie doesn't sit well with me, and I realize that if Scout and I are going to be friends, she's going to have to change her narrative about Cassie.

I let out a heavy sigh. "Listen, I know she's your aunt and you have stuff to sort out in your life, but I happen to like her."

"Yeah, ok. I was just kidding anyway."

I scan the kitchen. "Where are they?"

"She's playing cards at some friend's house, and Lyle decided to go fishing between rainstorms. Damn, does the weather around here know how to do anything else?"

"Not really."

"By the way, that was the strangest boat ride I've ever had in my life."

"You can say that again."

"Listen, Brooke," she starts, "I get that you're friends with some strange people, fine. And I know some heebie-jeebie crap went down on that boat. And Marcus's weirdo friend has definitely got some peculiars going on with him. But before we even get into all that, I have to tell you what happened to *me* last night."

"What?"

I can't make heads or tails of it either."

She stares at me as she wrings her hands. "I know there's things you can't tell me. That's fine; I get it. But this place here is starting to freak me out. There's a bag full of crazy everywhere I look in this town. And by the way, it's got the worst juju ever—I can feel it."

I nod. "Believe me, Scout, *I know*. Out with it."

Scout pushes through the front door and takes a seat on the porch, and I drop down next to her.

"Late last night, Cass and Lyle were sawing logs in the other room. God, it was annoying. Woke me right out of a sound sleep. And I couldn't get back to it, either, so I went downstairs, thinking I would find something to eat. Might as well, I'm up, after all, you know." She stares out over the lawn. "So, here I am, rummaging around in the fridge, and I hear the strangest noises coming from the kitchen, at the front door. It sounded like someone scratching, and I thought maybe it was that long tree branch, you know the one that likes to annoy the door every time we open it? God, I wish Lyle would trim it. Anyways, I thought it was that, but it wasn't."

A chill runs through me, and I almost don't want to ask. "Well, what was it then?"

"I don't know what it was. But right away, I saw him. He was standing on the other side of her screen door looking in. *Scary as hell!* And what are the odds that he would be standing there right as I woke up? It's like he appeared out of nowhere."

My stomach tightens. "What did he want?"

"I was just so startled and shocked to see him standing there, I asked him what he wanted. And at first, he wouldn't say."

"Did you let him in?"

"Hell no, I didn't let him in! But it's just a screen door. I'm sure he could have busted the latch quite easily."

"Creepy!"

"Damn straight, it was. Believe me, it left me shaking. I didn't know what to do. All this rain coming down in buckets, and he's standing there like he couldn't give two hoots. We had the longest stare down ever." She takes a breath. "Then he starts asking about Aunt Cassie."

"What did he say?" I ask, my mouth dry.

"Well, for one, he's not big on humor," she answers. "I said if he wanted to talk to Cassie, he'd have better luck visiting during the daylight hours, like everybody else. But when I go to close the door, he holds his creepy little hands up. Tells me to *make sure* I tell Cassie that he stopped on by. Like I'm gonna forget something like that! I swear to God, if the Prick were still here, he would have blown his head clear off."

I look over at her. "Did they already leave?"

"They left the day after the boat ride. My mom hates all the mosquitos, and the Prick said he didn't like it much here, either."

The Prick has good intuition.

"Do you miss your mom?"

She stares off in the distance. "You know, I probably should, but not really. The Prick would have been good to have around with these things slithering everywhere. Anyway, I go and lock the door because Mr. Creepy has left, or vanished, or went back to whatever rock he crawled out of. Good riddance, because I need to try and get some sleep. But as I'm dozing off, the next weird thing happens."

"Okay."

She sucks in another breath. "At first I thought I was in some kind of dream, you know, the lucid kind? Anyway, I'm pretty sure it was her."

I blink. "Who?"

"Ethel. I dreamed about Ethel."

"Ethel?"

Scout rubs at one of her scratches, making it bleed.

"Scout, you should get a bandage on that."

She huffs. "I don't need a damn bandage. I need to know what the hell is going on around here!" She gazes at me through tears in her eyes.

My throat feels tight. Even in death, Ethel can't seem to leave Cassie or the town of Neelsville alone.

"Oh, Scout, there's crazy stuff here for sure. But are you positive it was Ethel? I mean, you've never met her—what would she want from you?"

"I know what she looks like, Brooke," she scoffs. "I mean, take a look around—it's a damn shrine for her around here."

I glance at all the pictures Cassie put up of the two of them. They are peppered throughout the house. There is only one of her and Lyle.

"Okay, so you dreamed about her . . . ?"

"Yeah. At first, she was nice, floating around all smiley—like an angel, you know? Then she turns into this ugly, demon-like thing. Two seconds later, she's on my bed, on top of me, her face grotesque. She starts scratching at me, and that's when I punch her in the face. These are all from her."

My heart sinks. *How can we possibly combat that?*

"That's when I woke up. Ever hear of a dream doing that?"

"No."

Her face is pleading. "What is going on?"

She clearly wants more. But where do I start?

I clear my throat. "I'm afraid, Scout, that life here . . . it isn't what you think it is."

"Oh, gee whiz—ya think? Don't you think I got some sort of clue after that crazy-ass boat ride?"

My shoulders drop as I sigh. "Listen, there are bad things here."

"No, duh."

"I'm still trying to figure out what to do about them, I just haven't figured it out yet."

"Is the town full of them?"

I nod. "Enough to worry about. Marcus, the guy on the boat, he's on our side. And Aaron, his brother . . . he's the one that's missing. He was, well, sort of my boyfriend."

Scout's eyes meet mine. "Aaron?"

What can I say? I didn't exactly want to talk about it.

"Oh my God. That other guy on the boat—he's in on it, too, right? You dirty dogs, I knew something was off about him."

"He's just another supernatural, Scout. His name is the Traveller."

"'Just another supernatural'? Jesus. How do keep all that to yourself?"

"Good question. I don't really have a choice." I lean forward, grabbing her hand. "You can't mention anything about this to anyone, not even to Cassie."

"I won't. As long as you let my drinking today slide. I'll stop watering down her booze, I promise. Besides, I think she's on to me."

"Well, good. You don't need that stuff anyway." I take a breath and lean back into my seat. "I'm pretty sure half the town is infected. And I don't know—I knew Ethel for so long, and to see what happened to her.... It's hard to believe in anything after that."

"We can figure this thing out. Although part of me wants to hitch-hike back down to Florida. Except I can't stand it there, either."

"As long as we're on the subject—what's the deal with you and some mayor?"

Scout rolls her eyes. "*Oh, Gawd.* She told you, didn't she? You know, I love Cassie and all, but she's got the biggest mouth in the universe."

I nod, knowing all too well about Cassie and her big mouth.

"Well, it's not that big of a deal. He just likes buying me lunch sometimes. There's this great little restaurant he takes me to that's got the best cheeseburgers. And whenever women pass by our table, they give me the stink eye. But I don't pay it any mind, I know they're just jealous."

"Whoa, hold on." I put up my hand. "How did you even meet him?"

"Can't remember, really. I think I was at one of his rallies. Oh, yeah—he had some god-awful piece of food stuck right in his front teeth. Can you believe that? And wouldn't you know it, even with all those assholes around him, no one says a thing. I had no problem telling him, though."

"Um, how would you go about doing something like that?"

"It's not rocket science, Brooke. I was just standing near him and said 'Hey, you might want to check out a mirror; you've got food in your teeth. Unless you wanna walk around like Bozo the clown, you outta fine some floss.'"

"And from there, a deep friendship is born." I laugh.

Scout snorts. "Well, okay there, Mother Theresa, so what? Maybe he's got no one else down there to talk to. The thing is, I listen to people. All of the women around there got their duck lips, bouncy ass boobs, and heads in the clouds. Not a lick of sense, I tell ya, and they could care less about him—all they want really is his money. Funny thing, though . . . I think he knows, but he doesn't care. Besides, he likes buying me stuff for school and everything, so it's all good."

I raise an eyebrow. "It's all good?"

Scout shoots daggers from her eyes. "Look, you'd have to be one stupid son of a bitch to try something with me. I can more than handle myself."

"I don't doubt it for a minute, Scout."

"Besides, if Mom is so worried, why does she let me go see him—or come here, for that matter? That's what I mean about her being crazy."

I smile. "Well, Scout, for what it's worth, I'm glad you're here. But please, get some disinfectant on those scratches. They look infected."

"Yeah, I probably should." She sighs. "I swear, if I dream like this again, I'm gonna hitchhike back to Florida."

I think about Scout as I meander back home. I'm so grateful that she's here, and that I have someone to talk to. I feel better now that someone else knows—well, someone human.

Is she in more danger now that she knows? If she is, it will be my fault.

And how was I going to live with that?

Marcus is going to have to figure out something quick. He needs to come up with a plan, because I sure didn't have one.

THE VISIT

Margie

*M*argie is about done for the evening, wiping down the last cocktail table, when in comes a stray ten minutes before close. *Wouldn't you know it.*

God, how she hated that.

Her back is to the door, so she can't see who it is, but she knows it can't be anyone local. Everyone that lives around here knows she is pretty punctual when it comes to closing down her bar, especially during the week.

She hears the stranger's question before she sees him. "You still open for a few minutes, right?"

"Yeah, but I close in the next five."

The voice doesn't register with her, but as she turns around, she catches a glimpse of him in the doorway.

What??

She takes an instinctive step back. He's the last person she ever expected to darken her door.

He scans her up and down. "I thought I would come by for a visit. It's been a while since I've wandered into these parts."

He's tall and lean, dressed in all black, and looking like a thorny tree limb against the flocked red walls of her bar. Her plush chairs are arranged in a way that makes her customers feel at home. She prides herself on that. But his mere presence at the door has a way of sucking anything pleasant right out of existence. Funny, even in her own place, just seeing him standing there makes *her* want to leave.

She shakes her head to clear it.

Get a hold of yourself.

Her dogs are out in the backyard, and she wishes she hadn't let them out so soon. Her skin is clammy, and she's trying her best to put on a brave face.

But she couldn't hide all of her fear.

A chill has filtered in, and along with it, the strong smell of pine needles. She remembers that smell.

"Charming place you have here."

"That's how we like it. Listen, I can get you a drink, but you'll have to be quick about it. I like closing my bar on time."

The thing appraises her and flashes a grin. "Direct. I like that in a woman. So, what's good to drink?"

Look asshole, you better learn how to drink fast.

His weak attempt at charm was not going to work.

Not in this lifetime, buddy.

"We have several different beers, sir; take your pick."

"Why don't you surprise me then?"

She nods. He will have to do with a Miller Lite—she didn't want to turn her back to him. She pops the cap off and slides the bottle over, hyperaware that his eyes are watching her every move.

"You don't remember me, do you?"

She very much remembers him, but she's not going to give him the satisfaction of knowing that. That memory is the reason she wants to jump out of her own skin right now.

And from the looks of it, he hasn't changed one bit. In fact, he looks *exactly* the same as he did *twenty years ago*. But this time, she hopes he'll keep his sunglasses on. She doesn't think she can handle looking into those eyes again.

As long as she is aboveground, she will never forget the long twig of a man that walked into her place smelling like a rotten Christmas tree and ordering a Rob Roy. Their strange encounter—oh, so long ago—has never left her.

"I'm wondering if you could be of some service to me," he states after a long pull of his beer.

She absently scratches at her neck—just the simple act of talking with him is making her itchy. "Oh?"

"I'm looking for a young lady. I'm sure you know of her; she lives close by. I went over to her house earlier this evening, but she wasn't home."

"And who might that be?"

"A Ms. Brooke Larkin?"

Margie sucked in a breath. "What do you want with her?"

"Well, I'm sorry, but I'm not inclined to elaborate. It's sort of a private matter."

He wants to inquire about Brooke but will not say why. That's not shady at all.

He grins at that and takes another long swig of his beer. How can he possibly think she will tell him anything about Brooke?

And what "private matter"?

"It would be to her benefit to get in touch with me. We have reason to believe that there are malicious people after her."

"Malicious people? From where?"

"I'm sorry, but I'm not at liberty to discuss it. It would put everyone around here in danger. But if you see her, please give her my card. It's very important that I speak with her."

He slides a business card across the bar in her direction. The surface is a shiny black, and there's a phone number at the bottom, it's embossed in red font. She looks it over, thinking the obvious.

This looks like the devil's business card.

"That sounds pretty strange Mr. We don't have people like that in this town."

Margie doesn't know what to say, but she'll say anything to get him to leave.

"I'll pass this along."

"Good."

He finishes his drink and gets up from his barstool, taking a long look around.

"Amazing. This place hasn't changed a bit. Even the same color on the walls, I see. Remarkable."

He walks over and drags the tips of his fingers along the wall, a crooked smile on his face. His fingers remind her of a dead skeleton. *God, just leave already.* He stares at the walls of her place for a few moments.

"Looks like these could use a good scrubbing down, just not today." He laughs. "You have a great rest of the evening."

That will so not be happening.

"You, too, sir."

Calling him 'sir' makes her skin crawl. 'Thing' would be more accurate. She holds her breath as he glides out the door, and she has never been more thankful for anything in her entire life.

She waits a few seconds before rushing to the door and locking it behind him. Not that locks will help.

She sprints for the phone, it shakes in her hands as she dials a familiar number.

"Come on, pick up, pick up," she mutters as it rings in her ear.

Finally, the line picks up. "Hello?"

She exhales loudly, her whole body relaxing. "Cassie?"

"Yes, ma'am."

"Um, you remember the conversation we had about that funny looking guy that walked in here all those years ago?"

There's a long pause, so long that Margie thinks her friend may not have heard her.

"Cassie?"

"You mean, Mr. Pine Needles? The one that ordered a Rob Roy?"

"Yes."

"What of him?"

"Well, he's back."

Cassie sighs through the phone. "He's probably the same person who's been poking around here, bothering my niece in the middle of the night."

"Oh, God. What are we gonna do?"

"You need to call your sister, Margie."

A sharp pain shoots through her stomach. The time has been coming, but she knows she can't put it off any longer.

"Listen, Cassie," Margie says. "I'll be over in a few minutes."

BABYSITTING

Brooke

*B*abysitting isn't high on my list of things to do, but I could really use the money, and having some cash in my pocket never hurts. Mom is the town crier when it comes to hiring out my babysitting services—she can find me clients so fast my head spins.

Crap. I didn't feel like doing this tonight, but so be it.

As we make our way down the dirt driveway to the Smith's house, I can see their barn, it sits behind their house and looks like something straight out of a horror flick. And behind that, stands a windmill.

Even though their place gives off a whole lot of creepy vibes, as people, they've always been nice. They work with my dad at the Harley Davidson plant.

"All right, have fun."

Sure, mom. Not like I'm going to a party.

She drives off, leaving a swirl of dust in her wake. She loves her Country Squire station wagon, and drives that thing like there's no tomorrow. It has a V8 engine, so she can peel out of driveways with gusto.

She's halfway down the long drive before I make my way to the front door.

Mrs. Smith answers. "Come on in."

I follow her in and notice Mr. Smith, staring at himself in the mirror. He's a lanky man dressed in tight jeans and cowboy boots. The boots make his feet look absurdly long.

I zone out as the couple starts talking a mile a minute, prattling on about their plans for the evening.

I survey the room, noticing they've added to their collection of taxidermied animals. A new one is sitting on the coffee table, which is an upright squirrel. They still have the raccoon on top of the TV, and it's staring right at me. If I'm going to watch TV tonight, that thing will need to move. I don't understand how people can have animals preserved this way, placing them around their house like it's a dead zoo, but to each their own.

It's an old house, and I see there's a layer of dust everywhere, even on the stuffed animals.

I notice the sink is full of dirty dishes as we walk into the kitchen, and I wonder if she's expecting me to wash them. She gives a half-hearted smile.

"Oh, sorry. I haven't had a chance to get to those yet."

"Oh, that's okay."

The last thing I want to do is judge. I don't know the first thing about being a mother and looking after a family.

I watch as she picks up a used diaper off the counter, and I'm glad she does. She walks it over to the trash can, which was jam-packed, and shoves the diaper in there as best she can.

"I'll take that out later—don't you worry about it," she says.

Thank God.

"By the way, Brooke, there's plenty of food in the fridge. Help yourself to anything."

"Okay, thanks."

I brought my own snacks, and tonight is no different. I've never felt comfortable eating someone else's food, even if I'm the babysitter.

"Try to get the girls down by 8:30."

I nod politely. "Will do."

They have two girls, eight and eleven, and both are peeking out from behind their mother's legs.

"I can read a couple books to them."

"That'd be great. There's a few on the night-stand. It may be a late night."

"That's okay. Have a good night."

I watch from the front door as they climb into their car and drive off. The girls immediately run back to their room and resume playing on the floor with their dolls.

I turn on the TV, moving the raccoon. I happen to catch an episode of a late-seventies romantic comedy. I watch as the pretty Cruise Director manages to smooth over some sort of miscommunication with vacationers that have gotten in another cheesy predicament.

Then it's a show about a private investigator catching bad guys in Hawaii.

I glance down at my watch after several episodes have gone by. Eleven thirty.

I dread the next half hour and brace myself for the midnight static that graces all our TVs in Neelsville. I know it's coming, and it's the worst part of babysitting. I usually feel better having some kind of noise in the background.

Since the girls went down for bed surprisingly easy—they are already sleeping—I think that maybe I should do their dishes. The Smiths sure seem like they could use the help. There are several cereal bowls left over from the morning—well, *a* morning, because given how strongly pieces of cereal are stuck on the bowls like cement, I'd wager they've been here for a couple days.

I turn on the hot water and drizzle a generous amount of dish soap across the bowls. They definitely need to soak.

I can't stop thinking about what happened on the boat ride, about those crazy birds. Their eyes were the strangest shade of purple. But the worst part was that they didn't seem to be afraid of anything.

And that *thing*, Avalone. Good God—how are we going to deal with him?

Marcus better start showing himself soon.

I push aside the dirty curtains and notice again the red barn out behind the house, looking like a gust of wind could blow it down. And about fifty yards beyond that, the windmill sits, unassuming.

Funny, I know the woods around this whole area, and I didn't remember a windmill ever being there.

THE WINDMILL

Marcus

he lovely pull of the windmill keeps Marcus in tune with the rest of his body. It's always this way when you first step inside—it's a magical, mythical place, and the pull of it is already trying to manipulate his mind.

I know what you're doing, he thinks to himself.

The longer a person stays inside, the more the edges of reality will start to fold in on itself, getting mixed up with the realm of the distractors. He doesn't have much time to find Aaron's note. If his brother left any form of communication, he'll find it here.

And he's ready for whatever they're going to throw at him. Marcus knows that Brooke is only a short distance away, so maybe he can find some good news about Aaron and let her know.

But he wasn't expecting this.

Aaron left a message, all right. He scans the area, and senses it, high up on the wall. He knows the number; their kind has that particular trademark. He just needs to reach it with his mind.

His ancestors taught him all about windmills and how to handle them, so he knows what to do. And as he does, he can see the thoughts of countless others swirling about. He does his best to ignore them.

He catches the edges of the note, pulls it in, and carefully unfolds the outer envelope with his mind. He knows he has to pay close attention to what he's doing, not make any sudden moves, or he'll risk losing the entire note.

Once the envelope is open, he reaches for it, carefully pulling it in front of him with his hand. He does this with care; he doesn't want to lose the contents of the note forever.

He breaks the seal inside and unfolds the note.

> *Marcus,*
>
> *I'm glad you found my letter. But unfortunately, if you have, you know I didn't make it. Please don't stay in here long, Marcus—you know what happens when you do. Give Brooke all my love, and let her know that I sure tried. My love will always be with her, despite what is in me now. These circumstances were beyond my control, brother, and you know how dangerous the distractors can be. I'm so sorry I ended up getting captured. I let you down, and I let the innocent people of Neelsville down.*
>
> *I can't say it was a mistake coming to Neelsville, because I met her there. But now, because of that, they're all over the place. Dumb move, really. They are tricky, Marcus.*

Marcus reads every line as fast as he can, knowing he only has a few more minutes.

> *Please don't blame me, Marcus, and don't try looking for me. A part of me will always love my family and Brooke, despite what I am. I'm just thankful that I finally experienced what*

real love is, brother, if only for a short time. But I felt it, and it's the best feeling in the world.

I mean what I said about you trying to find me. Things will go badly for any of you if you try. Marcus, I hate to say this, but you know I'm one of them now. Leaving this message has taken the last shred of our kind out of me—you know this kind of thing just accelerates the process.

Please remember me as I used to be. If we meet again, you know what you must do. It will be the best thing for both of us. Believe me, I'll put up a fight, but deep down, I'll be glad you had the courage to destroy what I've become.

Please give my love to Brooke, and let her know that I'm sorry things turned out this way. In love and peace,

Aaron

Marcus reread the last line, feeling empty. *Love and peace? What a complete jackass.*

Marcus screams. "Aaron!" He falls to the ground, sobbing. He has to get out of here—it won't be long before their penetrating thoughts will start sinking into his skull. Even as a supernatural, he's not impervious to it.

As he turns to leave, he realizes that he isn't alone. Someone is standing to his right. And he's seen him before.

Ah, yes. The funeral.

It's that damn doctor from the med center, Peter, is here, and there's no good reason for him to be. He attended Ethel's funeral, for what, God only knows. Probably out scouting around for more souls.

Marcus can smell his disease, the doctor's every pore is oozing out the infected virus. He glances his way.

Marcus breaks the heavy silence between them. "What do you want?"

"Do you really have to ask?" The doctor grins, his shoulders heaving in a heavy sigh. "For a higher being, you guys are always a day late and a dollar short. What's become of your race? I thought you were *supreme beings*?"

Marcus thought this may happen. He just didn't think it would be this soon.

"You're too late, Marcus. And it's starting with you, I'm afraid."

Marcus knows this, and yet he is fighting it with everything he has.

"I'm coming for her, Marcus. She's going to be mine."

Like a punch to the gut, Marcus knows he's talking about Brooke.

I need to warn her. He knows she is in grave danger. Except he can't get any of his limbs to move.

He cannot let the doctor get to her, and she isn't far from here. It will be easy to . . . Shit, this is all so impossible. It won't be long before the doctor finds all this out.

Marcus gathers all his mental strength to block the distractor from entering his thoughts, but he's at his most vulnerable inside this windmill.

"I think you and your brother need to realize who's boss."

"You're a disgusting race," Marcus shot back, unable to help himself. "You always have been."

"We have big plans for Aaron—too bad you won't be able to see it."

Marcus uses all his strength to fight him off. His brain feels like it's drowning in quicksand. He's close to passing out, and when he does, Brooke will surely be captured. And if that happens, he will never forgive himself.

He can read all the emotions coming from the doctor, and Peter is hellbent on Brooke.

She won't have a chance.

But he can do one thing, he isn't about to let the doctor get the best of him. It won't be long now before he will be manipulated completely, and he fights it with everything he has.

"So, first things first, where is she?"

Marcus concentrates with all his might, but he's so much weaker now. He scans the room for a way out, but there isn't one. And slowly, ever so slowly, he feels the doctor entering his mind. It feels like someone turned on a faucet of cold water and it was now slowly pouring into his brain. *God, it was cold.*

"Kinda icy, isn't it?"

Marcus scowls up at him from where he's collapsed against the wall.

"Think of it as a minor tweaking—a brain purification, if you will."

"You're the one with the disease."

Marcus holds on as long as he can, the river of cold snaking its way through his mind.

"Don't worry; it won't be long now. I'm finding things out as we speak." The doctor perks up. "Ah, what do we have here? Interesting."

Marcus longs to move, but he's stuck. The trail of cold is freezing every synapse of his brain, migrating through his pathways. Soon, he'll be nothing but ice.

Well, if he's gonna turn anyway . . . "It's kind of funny, you know, the way you think of her."

The doctor's nostrils flare as his eyes flash. "Oh, really?"

"She doesn't think of you that way. She never will, but good luck."

"I won't be needing any luck when I'm done with her. She will eventually see reason."

Marcus's stomach rolls knowing that his thoughts will lead this man to Brooke. He gathers every last bit of strength he has, pulls out his sword, and throws it in the direction of the doctor. It sticks in his arm, and he doesn't even flinch.

"Are you kidding me? She's just down the road?" He throws his head back as he laughs. "I can't tell you how fun this is going to be. Too bad you won't be able to see it, really."

"You're delusional; she'll never want to be with you."

The doctor pulls out the spear with ease. "And you think this is going to stop me?" Dark laughter fills the air. "You guys are hilarious. I almost feel sorry for you."

"It's going to take a lot more than this to stop us. And by the way, in the next five minutes, you're going to want to chase her right along with me. You know it, and I know it."

Marcus is done listening to him. He presses his hands on the cement, pushing up with all his might, but his arms shake, and he falls. The spell of the windmill is too great.

He's not in charge of himself, not anymore. He can feel himself turning.

Peter hisses in his direction. "It's not that bad, and it's only for eternity. Let it go."

Marcus tries punching at the doctor, but he knows it's useless. He does what he can with the last few seconds he still has as himself. He pushes to his feet, using the last bits of his strength, and lurches toward the exit. He knows she can't hear him, but he yells her name anyway, stumbling out into the night air.

"Brooke!"

AN AWAKENING

He collapses just outside the windmill, hoping that enough of him got out of its range. Before he loses consciousness, he crawls as far away as he can manage. His last coherent thought echoes through his muddled brain before the world goes dark. *I hope I don't wake up as a distractor.*

☽

SMELLING THE ROSES

Dr. Cooper

he doctor, the distractor, needs to tend to his arm. The cut won't leave a scar, but having blood everywhere is no good for anybody, and he's making a mess. He needs bandages, and quick.

He has a brilliant idea. And this is perfect; his wound will make the perfect alibi.

According to Marcus's thoughts, Brooke is fairly close. He sniffs at the air, turning his head toward the nearby farmhouse right off the road. *Of course.* He hurries off in that direction, well aware that the wildlife around him has turned silent.

As he walks, he muses, stopping to smell the roses, as it were. The evening hour is so beautiful. He never had time to appreciate it when he was full human; he was either on call or working. But tonight, the sky is full of twinkling stars, and alive with fireflies.

He loves how his distractor traits enhance the senses. He's aware that his presence amongst the trees quiets every living thing in the area as he passes—*and it feels so good to reign supreme.*

Being a distractor is starting to suit him. If one of his kind feels particularly fond of someone, the emotional impact is exponential, a hundred times stronger than humanly possible. This is dangerous, because he's still trying to figure out how to control it himself.

Sometimes his emotions make him feel like an animal. *Primal.*

He can detect her heartbeat now, he must be getting into range. He eyes the farmhouse down the hill. What are the odds that she would be babysitting here tonight?

Every human has a distinct personal chime to them, a melody. As a human, it's impossible to detect. But for a distractor, it's the first thing they notice. Along with the human's smell, the chime serves as a calling card of sorts. And right now, hers is calling to him like a siren song.

Just a few more steps.

He's going to have to figure out what to say to her. He'll need to choreograph this dance carefully. He doesn't want her intentionally getting hurt, and he doesn't want to give everything away, not just yet.

A slight breeze picks up, and he starts to sense her smell in the air, making him high.

He can taste her.

He's starting to crave her now, the desire in him reaching a boiling point. This is why he feels like an animal—this primal urge, *need*, for something outside himself is all-consuming.

Relax, take a deep breath.

He glances over at the bright Harvest Moon sitting low in the sky, noticing how its shadow plays across the edges of the forest, casting everything in its warm glow.

He turns his attention back to the situation at hand. Brooke probably won't leave willingly, so he needs to find some rope. Farmers usually have some around, right? He takes a quick detour toward the barn to see what he can find.

THE RACE

Brooke

*I*t's the devil's hour, and the gray static from the TV is so loud, it awakes me from a sound sleep. The last time I was here, the only dead, taxidermied animal was the deer head on the wall. Now their whole living room was teaming with stuffed wildlife. And it looks like they're all watching me.

This is going to be a long night.

I lift off the couch and turn on the radio on a shelf nearby, fumbling with the knob. *Why isn't anything coming in?* Strange, we're just a mile down the road, and we can always get at least one station to work.

Maybe there's another storm brewing.

I hate not having any noise. I amble around the house, trying to find anything that could drown out any sounds from the house, creaks or anything else.

I peek my head into the bedroom; and see the girls are fast asleep. I walk back to the kitchen and over to the fridge to scrounge around for something to eat. The clock reads 12:06, it's one of those old-fashioned kinds in the shape of a black cat whose tail and eyeballs move with each second that passes. Last time I was here, the Smiths didn't come walking through the door until three.

I have a long evening ahead of me.

I spy a perfectly ripe banana and check to make sure it hasn't been peed on by cats. They have at least three of them wandering around, and every once in a while, I get a whiff of cat urine.

I'm hoping Marcus might pay me a visit; it sure would be nice to have him here right now. I have so many questions about what happened on that boat. He has a way of making me feel at ease, even if he doesn't want to—or can't—tell me everything. He says he will find a way to beat these things, but then again, Aaron told me the same thing.

I stop in the hallway, thinking I heard something at the door.

Who would be knocking at this hour?

I venture out of the kitchen and into the foyer, turning towards the door. I see someone standing there through the windows and I'm excited because I first think it's Marcus.

Good Lord, I hope it's not that needle of a man asking Scout about Cassie the other day. *Why would anyone come here at midnight?*

"Brooke? Is that you?"

I'm surprised by the familiar voice, and as I pull back the curtains, my eyes widen to see the doctor from the med center. He's holding his arm funny, like he's been hurt. I quickly unlock the door.

"What happened?"

"Just got in an accident down the road."

"Oh, come on in."

He gives me a big smile as he passes me.

"Just about got plowed over by some asshole."

I see that he's holding his arm at the elbow, and there's blood smeared all around it.

"Are you okay?"

"Yeah. I could use something to wipe this up, though. I don't want to get blood all over."

I jolt. "Oh, sorry, of course."

I launch into action, grabbing the nearest roll of paper towels from the kitchen. I offer him a couple for his arm.

"Thank you." He presses them to the wound and looks around. "You don't mind if I sit down, do you?"

"Of course not." I extend my arm toward the couch before we both take a seat. "Listen, don't you want to call the police?"

"I don't think so. He's probably long gone anyway," the doctor scans the room, a peculiar look on his face. "Wow! They've got a whole little forest full of animals going on in here."

"Don't I know it, it feels like they're all staring at me."

He chuckles. "Do you know these people well?"

"A little bit. Mr. Smith works with my dad. They're pretty chill."

"Well, that's good. I wouldn't want them freaking out over a strange guy in their living room."

"I think they'd be okay with it, considering the circumstances."

"So, you were just driving down the road?"

"Yep, just minding my own business , and this car comes flying into my lane out of nowhere. If I hadn't swerved, I probably wouldn't be talking to you right now."

I cock my head to the side, noting how strange to have the doctor here, and in their living room, of all places.

"How scary! Say, do you want me to make you some coffee or something? Something hot?"

"I'm good. I've got enough adrenaline flowing to keep me up and kicking for the next few days."

I couldn't help but think back to my grandma and her ill-fated trip to Florida.

"Are you okay, Brooke?"

"Yeah, it's just . . .well, my grandmother was killed in a car accident."

"Oh, really? I'm sorry to hear that. How did that happen?"

"Drunk driver."

"Boy, sometimes you just never know."

"I know." I nod absently and straighten in my seat. "Anyway, that was a long time ago. Hey, um, are you sure you don't want to call the police? At least file a report?"

"That's not necessary, Brooke."

"Really? But what if he does it to someone else?"

"He won't, I assure you. Anyway, I want to show you something."

I couldn't believe he didn't want to call anyone.

"Show me what?"

"You see that animal over there, Mr. Raccoon?"

"Yeah, he's kinda hard to miss."

"What would you say if, well, I brought him back to life?"

I would think that maybe the good doctor might have bumped his head in the accident.

"Well, I know you're a doctor and all, but even doctors have limits." I flash him a nervous smile. *What is he saying?*

"Well, in my world, not so much."

I suddenly have the urge to get up. Like run away. Because something isn't right. "Did you just say 'in your world'?"

I recall then what Marcus had said about the doctor.

Oh God, how could I forget that?

He nods. "It's just preservation. And this here? It's all an illusion."

Okay, *please be joking.* But the knot in my stomach tells me he's not joking at all.

"What? Are you talking about the dead animals?"

"Would you believe me if I told you that I have the ability to bring them all back?"

My heart stutters. *What?!* "How could you possibly . . . ?"

I didn't want to believe it. Even in the midst of him starting this voodoo crap. I just didn't want to face it.

I watch as the doctor makes a strange face, snaps his fingers, and just like that, the taxidermied raccoon's head slowly starts to move from side to side. As it does, I feel nausea threatening. I need to get out of there, out of this room, but I can't; I'm frozen in place.

The squirrel on the coffee table starts mimicking the raccoon's movements, and soon all the dead animals are starting to move in a strange way.

I hiss in my anger, remembering to keep my voice down for the girls sleeping in the other room. **"What are you doing?"**

It becomes apparent to me that the raccoon is now, very much alive.

And Dr. Cooper is a distractor, and I just let him in the damn house.

The raccoon races across the floor with the squirrel and the other animals who've joined in the party. A few come scurrying out of the girls' open bedroom door, sniffing at the air, looking for a way out. All very much alive.

I jump up, sprinting towards the door to let them all out, and wanting to leave myself. But the kids are still in their bedroom.

I have to protect them.

I run through the kitchen, throw open the front door, and let all the freaky Lazarus animals out. I'm glad that at least, they got away. *I won't be that lucky.*

The doctor is on me in two seconds, pushing me hard into the door. He grabs my arms, holding me against the wood, and leans in. I'm shocked by his aggressiveness, his face mere inches from mine. He whispers in my ear. "There are so many things I want to show you, Brooke. And that was just a little taste."

Is this really happening? "I'm not interested."

"Oh, but you will be. This world is too colorful to experience alone. I need someone to stand with me."

"I let you in because I thought you needed my help." Deep down, I know my attempt at reasoning with him is futile, but I still try.

"I do. I do need your help, Brooke. We could be such a great team together."

"How so? To hurt people? Well, good for you, but I'm not into that."

"Look at my arm," he pleads, extending it between us while tightening his grip with his other arm so I couldn't get away. "No blood."

The gash on his arm was already healing. And the only thing that could do that was a supernatural, or, in this case, a *distractor.*

"I don't even want to know how you got this way, and I don't want any part of it."

"If you know what I am, why not just say it out loud?"

"I don't want to."

I hate that he's standing so close, it feels like he wants to smother me.

"Go ahead. In fact, I want you to."

He's waiting for me, but I'm too terrified to speak. My voice is barely a whisper.

"You're a distractor. There, is that what you want?"

"Very good." He sniffs my hair. "Good grief, it's been too long."

"Why won't you let me go?"

"That's not possible. You know how hard this is for me right now? All the things I want to do with you just swirling about in my head."

I can't believe this. How am I going to get out of here?

"You should give me some credit, actually; I think I'm doing a pretty good job, considering."

I'm trembling, and I can't stop it.

"You're lucky I haven't done anything to you yet."

I try pleading. "If you let me go, I won't say anything."

His creepy laugh rings throughout the Smiths' dirty, pee-ridden house. "I don't need your empty words, Brooke. Christ, you're such a liar. But I already knew this about you."

Just then, one of the family's cats strolls in, its back arched, and hisses at the doctor.

He hisses back, and it scampers out of the room. "What evil creatures they are."

"What do you want?"

His sharp laugh pierces the air. "Do you even have to ask?"

Pain slices through my stomach.

"You would make such a beautiful distractor. You know that, don't you?"

A shudder runs through me as I think of myself as one of them.

He leans into my ear and whispers, "Tell you what. I'm going to let you walk out of this house, and I'll even give you a head start. You can run wherever you want to."

"Head start for what?"

"Now be sensible, Brooke. There are kids in the other room, so you need to keep quiet."

"Leave them alone," I grit out.

"I can assure you, I will. But before you go, I will need to bind your hands."

"Why?"

"I'm asking you to, that's why."

He quickly reaches into his pocket, pulls out a line of rope, and ties it around my wrists before I can do anything else. I just stand there, shaking in his presence. He runs his hand through his hair, while the other has a good grip on both of my shackled hands, keeping me in place.

"That should do it."

"I'll scream if you touch me again."

He starts laughing again. "And risk waking up the kids? Remember, be smart."

"Leave the kids out of it. Even a ghoul like you should realize they haven't done anything."

He lets out an exasperated sigh. "Listen, you really should be worrying more about yourself."

I stand there, my hands tied behind me, agreeing to his demands. I know he won't want to deal with the kids, so I send up a silent prayer that they stay asleep.

"I'm curious to see how far you'll get."

"You're sick."

"It will be a fun game for the both of us. I want to see how long it takes me to find you. Think of it as a game—I'll even time it. I'm guessing I'll be hot on your trail in under two minutes. I could be wrong, though; you seem rather efficient. It may take three. But rest assured, *I will find you.*"

He lets go of me and steps us back, pulling open the front door. "Ladies first."

Reluctantly, I step outside. I glance over my shoulder at him from the porch. "I let you in because I thought you needed help. But all you are is a monster."

He whips me around to face him as his eyes narrow fiercely, and barks out, "I'd watch your mouth if I were you."

I take a small step backward as he steps closer. I almost fall, but he grabs me, standing me up.

"You see, I'm good for you, Brooke. And let's face it; you could use some looking after."

I shake him off. "I don't think so."

I sense my time on this porch is coming to an end. I scan my surroundings, looking for the quickest way into the woods.

"That's right; go there. It's only my little sanctuary, and I know every trail there is. But good luck to you." His lips curl up in a snarl. "Think of it as the ultimate game, Brooke; your life depends on it. Your real life, with me."

He checks his watch. "I'm going to give you five minutes, and the time starts, now."

I know his intentions are evil. And I know if I walk out, he will eventually catch me, but the kids will be safe. Yes, the door to the house will be unlocked, but they will be okay.

And he will soon find me, no matter how far I get.

But I have to try.

I start running toward the edge of the woods. I figure it's better than the field—at least in the woods I'll have cover. I glance back and can still see him standing at the door. True to his word, he hasn't left, not yet anyway.

"Ticktock, Brooke. Start running! At least make it interesting for me."

That's when I realize: My hands are tied, but my legs aren't.

He taunts me again. "Almost at a minute already; you should probably pick up the pace."

Where are those powers now that I need them?

But my powers are long gone, and I run as fast as I can.

I don't look back.

MAVIS ABERDEEN

Mavis

Mavis knew the day was going to be different by the ringing in her ears. It's rare that she gets a headache, so this one feels rather unusual. She wills herself out of bed, making her way to the kitchen window to peer outside. She can't decide between mint or lavender tea, but settles on the latter.

Her dog will not stop barking. "I know, I know. You wanna treat?" She grabs the box off the counter and pulls out a dog biscuit. He carefully takes the tiny treat with his mouth.

She opens the fridge, thinking it's going to be a bacon-and-eggs kind of day—something tells her she'll need the extra protein. The light in her fridge isn't working, but that's no problem. She whispers a quick chant and carries on.

She'll never tire of her special abilities that help make her day more manageable. At this point in her life, they are essential.

She un-wraps the sticky bacon and carefully places each one in her cast-iron skillet. She hates it when bacon is underdone in parts, so she has her routine down. Soon the mouth-watering smell flows throughout the kitchen, softening her mood.

She hears the ringing again. Good Lord, what a foul time to be having a migraine. If her intuition is correct—and it almost always is—she'll need to be firing on all cylinders today.

As the bacon finishes up, she catches a glance out the window and sees shades of a mustard-colored sky. She hears the whispers of her oversized flowers, and it sounds like a lullaby. This isn't anything new. She can hear the thoughts of any living being—and they always let her--giving her carte blanche, permission to inundate their mind.

That permission extends to plants and animals. Sometimes she turns it off—she doesn't care to let all that noise in, it tends to wreck-havoc in her brain. And the last thing she needs when she wants to relax with a book.

But mundane as it is, sometimes it's nice to have a buffer against all the chaos that is in Mavis's brain.

Without that simple diversion, she feels she'll explode. Thoughts from things that swim in the lake are neither exciting nor compelling, just the inner rumblings of where they are getting their next meal or where they plan to lay their eggs. But they do bring a welcome comfort.

The birds are the best; they have such vibrant imaginations. Whoever thought of the word "birdbrain" to describe a stupid person, well, they couldn't have been farther off base.

Her mind turns to the dark crow pecking away at the ground near her window. She notices that the feathers of some of the birds in the area are darkening. They are changing, ever so slightly, and she's killing them just as soon as they are starting to turn, but she can't get them all.

She knows their bad news.

She knows this is the work of the pests trying to penetrate the area, the first phase of their evil plan. They want to take over everything.

Just then, the crow looks up, watching her intently. Birds have always been harbingers of the spirit world, translating and delivering messages and feelings from the dead. She can often see these messages, especially from those that have just passed. It isn't really a special gift of hers—humans just have to be open enough to see it for themselves.

Mavis is well aware of the ten-day waiting period afforded to humans that have died and are not yet ready. One last human indulgence to roam about, to visit places that they may never have seen in life, but had wanted to.

Some choose to watch over their loved ones a bit longer, a sort of hiccup or pause on their way to spiritual enlightenment. Mavis can often see them swirling about in other people's homes, in stores, outside even—the image is just as tangible as the bacon frying in her pan.

Sometimes they are a nuisance. She guides them when she can, but ghosts are hard to direct, they don't generally like being told what to do. Usually overwhelmed by the sudden drastic change to their circumstances, they are often unreliable, preferring to do things for themselves. *And that is the problem.*

Mavis thinks back to her brother-in-law. He was a curious sort. Salty in nature, but had that annoying ability to find the chink in one's armor.

In life, he always had a chip on his shoulder, preferring to indulge in discord, rather than biting his tongue. His soul craved adversity like a drug. His mother liked to say "He just came out that way, crying like the devil!"

Because of this innate sense, people either loved or hated him. He'd always had a bond with high-energy people, the misfits, the ones that regular society couldn't seem to relate to.

Shortly after he passed, she had been in her garden, recalling a conversation that they'd had about lawn sprinklers. He'd mentioned that if reincarnation was real, he would like to come back and use them to torture the heck out of some poor, innocent walker that just happened to pass on by.

She'd never forgotten that conversation, and while pruning her weeds, she got the odd sensation that she wasn't alone. She'd stood up and caught the last half of a gray mist floating about, hovering over her flower bed, and shortly after that, a sprinkler turned on full blast right in front of her, spraying her squarely in the face.

Mavis knew right away it was him. She screamed before she started laughing, which made her fall into a small pocket of mud in her garden. She was certain he was laughing at her from the great beyond.

It was a fitting last meeting, and something he would have planned out. She yelled out for him to get on with his light path already; he had things to do. He must have obliged, because she did not feel his spirit with her again after that day. She considered it both a privilege and an honor to get a visit from him, and she would never forget it.

Her thoughts are interrupted by the ring of her phone. Of course, she already knows who it is.

She answers the phone, the soft voice on the other end both familiar and unrecognizable. "Mavis?"

"Yes, dear?"

Her sister hesitates. Mavis knows her own sister is afraid of her. She can't blame her—she has given her plenty of reasons over the years. "Um, we've got some real problems around here."

"No kidding." She can't help the sarcasm that bites out in her reply.

"We need your help."

"I'm sure you do." An intense pain shoots through her chest right then, and she winces, rubbing at the spot. Instantly, she knows that someone she cares about is in real trouble. "These things are sneaky, Margie."

The pain isn't letting up, and at first, Mavis thinks she's having a heart attack. But then she realizes what this really is, *she is getting one of her signs.*

But she can't let her sister off the hook just yet. "How long since we've conversed? And I live just down the street. That's very rude of you, Margie."

"I know, Mavis, and I'm sorry."

"Something's wrong."

"I know that, Mavis. That's why I'm calling."

"Brooke is mixed up in some trouble." Mavis lets the pain spread—she knows it's the only way she'll be able to find her. Brooke is in real danger, she feels it in her soul.

"Mavis, we need to meet. You need to help me deal with these things."

"Let me come to you."

Margie sighs, and Mavis thinks she sounds relieved. "Okay."

Mavis hangs up the phone in a huff. She's annoyed at how uncomplicated 'regular humans' thoughts are, and this includes her sister. But she knows she can't help it. None of them can.

And that's why Mavis has to help.

THE CHIME

Brooke

I'm running across a scattering of twigs and stones, cutting up my bare feet, but I don't care. I want to get far, far away from here. I didn't have time to put on shoes, and I keep running in spite of the pain.

Getting up close and personal with one of those things has a way of making a person leave the room in a hurry.

Dr. Cooper is hideous on all fronts, but I feel sad for him, too. At one time or another, he'd been a good person. He had been a well-meaning doctor working in his chosen profession, because he'd wanted to help people.

But that doesn't change the fact that he is chasing me right now. I picture how the authorities will find my body out in the woods.

I sprint to the thickest part of the woods I can find, running right through all the thorny, berry bushes. Not that a few thorns will keep him away. My feet are bleeding, and of course, I trip.

It's not easy trying to get back up with my hands tied behind me, but I manage.

I pass by a little stream, taking note of the running water. This will make good cover for any noises I make, because so far, I've managed to crack every twig in the area.

I pause for a moment to get my bearings, and remember there's a cave not too far away. It's probably the first place he'll look, but I head for it anyway. I keep stepping on jagged rocks along the way, and it slows down my progress. I feel like everything in this woods wants me to be found.

I jerk to a stop, leaning up against a massive oak. I have to stop—I can barely breathe.

And that's when I notice it.

Everything in this surrounding woods is grey.

What was once a small, grey patch of grass only a minute ago has now grown all over the place. It looks like silvery snow in the moonlight.

What is going on?

I hear a branch snap several yards behind me, and my eyes shoot wide as I dart away from the tree. I've never been good at running, but now my life depends on it. *What a sick joke.*

I keep running, sprinting up hills and down gullies as fast as my lungs will physically allow. I am very aware that he's on my heels and will be here at any moment.

I hear things all around me, like someone has woke up every living thing in the woods—snapped twigs, crunchy leaves being stepped on, tree limbs breaking. I can't decipher if it's him or just a squirrel.

How could it have come to this?

I find the cave and make my way to it. I can't see anything in here—it's as dark as ink. My mind races as I catch my breath, and I don't know which is worse: me running from him, or me being caught.

Sweat is dripping off my forehead, and the salt stings my eyes. I wish my hands were free, I want so badly to wipe it. I scan the cave, hoping to find something sharp. No luck there—my eyes still haven't adjusted to the dark.

Maybe if I lie flat on the ground, I can buy some time. I remember Aaron telling me that the closer a person is to the ground, the harder it is for a distractor to detect them. He never said why that was.

He never said a lot of things.

As I lie there, arguing with myself, I try to figure out my next move. I wonder what that couple will think when they come home to no babysitter, front door open, knowing I left their girls all by themselves.

And I won't get a chance to explain.

I lie flat against the ground in the damp dirt, my bound hands awkwardly sticking out to one side so they don't fall completely asleep beneath me. I hear birds squawking outside the entrance of the shallow cave, and I notice a few of them sitting high up in a nearby tree. Their songs don't seem like anything a bird would sing. Especially not now, in the middle of the night.

I move around on the ground, and try to get a better view. And when I do, my heart stops.

The birds aren't singing any songs.

"I know about you," it chirps.

I blink, convinced the events of this night have made me go crazy.

I hear it again. "I know about you."

It's mocking me in a cold, childish tone, and I stare up at it. I find my voice to ask a one-word question. "What?"

"I know about you. I know about your grandma, and I know about you."

I'm frozen, unmoving, and I'm finding it hard to breathe.

This bird is talking to me.

"I'm just a bird, and I know about you," it singsongs. "I see everything, yes, I can."

I look up and see the glare of its eye from where it's perched high on a limb. And I recognize it—it's one of those fake-looking birds I saw on the boat. The ones with the purple eyes.

It starts in again with the awful words. "I know about your grandma."

Is this some kind of a sick joke?

It continues. "You don't know what I know. But I know everything."

"Who the hell are you?" I whisper as quietly as I can.

"I'm just a bird."

I hear footsteps nearby, and I shudder, knowing my pursuer is getting closer. He confirms it when his next words ring out through the still night. "I'm coming for you, Brooke."

Great. I've got some loony-tune bird talking shit to me and some whacked-out distractor who wants to do God knows what, all hot on my trail.

I crane my neck in the direction of the voice. He's close, and of course, the bird won't shut up. "She's over here, she is."

I get up from the ground, and run as fast as I can away from the cave and the bird from hell. The cave is no longer an option; that's the first place he'll look.

Get back on solid ground. After a few twist and turns, I find a spot that doesn't look covered in sharp rocks and wait.

"I can smell you in the air, Brooke."

I shudder as I lie back down on the ground.

"You're going to lead me right to you."

I don't dare move.

"I can hear your chime, and my God, it's perfection."

I start shaking in the dirt, cursing this impossible situation. *When will this bad dream go away?*

"It's such a distinct, pretty sound," the disembodied voice continues. "I sense the purity in it. It's like nothing else I've ever heard before."

I don't know what the hell he's talking about, but whatever he's hearing from me, I'm not sure what it is. And I can't turn off what I don't hear.

"I wish you could hear it; you would like it. It's telling me right now where to find you. See, there are parts of you, Brooke, that still want to be found."

His footsteps are closing in; he's not far now.

The ground is cold, and I dare not breathe. And where is that damn bird? I can hear it flying around in the trees, probably searching for me to give away my location.

I want to kill it.

And suddenly, as if I'd willed him to find me, the bird calls, "She's close by, she's close by."

I..Want. To. Kill. That. Damn. Bird.

I feel a rush of air as it swoops down—*oh crap*—and it starts pecking at my side. I scream at the thing, the bird from hell, trying to shoo it away. But my hands are still bound, and I can't defend myself. "Get away from me!"

It keeps coming at me with its jagged beak, pecking at me everywhere. I feel each jab, the stabbing pain compounding as it spreads all over.

I'm rolling around on the ground now, trying to avoid getting pecked, but it keeps coming back for more.

I want to rip the bird apart, but since my hands are shackled behind me, I kick at it. We're at eye level now, and its eyes are glowing a purplish white.

"I know about you."

It starts pecking at me again, going in for round two. And that's when the once-good doctor finds me.

When he sees the bird on top of me, he yells at the top of his lungs. "GET AWAY FROM HER!"

His screech scares everything within range. He picks up the bird, breaking its neck with ease and whipping the small carcass into the woods. I hear its body fly through the forest and it slams against the trunk of a nearby tree.

"Did it hurt you?"

I don't have to state the obvious; my mangled body says more than enough.

His eyes flash, his nostrils flaring. "Nooooo!"

My blood is all over the place, up my arms and down my sides. He hovers over me, his face pained.

"Let me help you." He kneels on the ground and gingerly picks me up, leaning me against a tree. He surveys my arms. "And you couldn't even defend yourself. I'm so sorry."

He unties my hands and holds them in his. I try pulling away, but his grip is strong.

"I want you to stand very still."

Okay. He grabs my wrist, and before I can do anything, he bends down and slowly starts licking my hand, my arm, his tongue tracing each and every wound. I just stand there against the tree, in a daze. I watch as he repeats this on the other arm, his touch gentle and caring.

He carefully lifts my bloodstained shirt, taking in all the peck marks at my side. Then he bends down and licks every single one.

I just stand there, not knowing how to feel. Dizzy, I guess, like I am about to pass out. "What are you doing?"

"I'm healing you."

"I don't want to be healed; I want to be left alone."

He whispers in my ear, "If I leave you alone now, Brooke, these infections will kill you. That, my dear, was a demon bird. And you can't leave these kind of wounds untreated."

As I listen to his words, a soothing balm comes over me. I can feel its numbing affect, working its magic into my legs and chest. It reaches up my neck, across my face, and into my head.

"How do you feel?"

I can hear my own words, but they sound muffled, far away. "I don't feel like me." My limbs feel heavy, like I'm floating underwater. I shake my head, trying to stay awake. "It's hard to hear; what is going on?"

"Are you still scared?"

"Whatever you're doing, please stop," I plead. "This isn't me."

His laugh echoes through the moonlit sky. "You don't know what your true self is until you become a distractor."

I feel the brush of his hand at the back of my neck, and he starts kissing the shell of my ear. He soon finds my lips, planting a small, tender kiss there, and I can't move. Then he stops and whispers in my ear. "Just a little kiss for now."

None of my extremities are working or even seem capable of it. He brushes my hair to the side and stares into my eyes. I see a glimmer in them.

"You're just feeling the anti-venom working its way into your nervous system; nothing to be alarmed about."

"You're not being fair," I shoot back, but it sounds half-hearted to my ears. It's the last thing I remember saying to him.

"Soon you'll be sleeping," he coos, and nausea rolls my stomach. "I'm going to take you away from all this."

He's so close I can hear him breathing as he picks me up. Then he speaks the last words I hear before passing out.

"Wait until they see what I've brought them."

KALEB'S DREAM

Kaleb

*K*aleb, can you hear me?

Kaleb hears soft words echo throughout his mind, as clear as day to him. He doesn't even question answering back. "Yes."

I'm in trouble.

He closes his eyes, searching deep within himself. Yes, he can feel it; someone he cares about is very much in trouble. He can read it in her chime—like a reverberating echo, it rings throughout his being.

But how can he hear her, and where is her voice coming from?

Ever since he signed the contract, he's acquired this new sense, and it is taking some getting used to.

Please, listen to me, the voice pleads.

"I want to help; where are you?"

Her answer chills him to the bone. *I am nowhere to be found.*

"What do you mean?"

You can't find me. Well, not on your terms anyway. I no longer exist. I am nothing, at least in the way that humans know.

But I'm no longer human, I reply.

Yes, you still are, Kaleb.

He doesn't know what to do with that. *I want to help you.*

The voice hesitates. *You can help me by finding Marcus.*

A heavy feeling washes over Kaleb, he suddenly feels an over-whelming need to know exactly where she is. He's worried for her. Worried for Brooke.

Funny, he still doesn't know much about her at all, but he feels like they'd met once before. And how can he feel everything that she's feeling?

He supposes he should be suspicious, but this doesn't feel like a trap. It just feels, well, *familiar*. Like home. And nothing about that makes sense.

You can't find me, Kaleb.

She's uncomfortable; he can tell. Is she underwater? Wherever she is, he can't see it. She's murky and out of focus, but he can feel her shaking. Wherever she is, she's cold.

But how is she communicating with him?

Do you remember the bridge, Kaleb?

He thinks back as far as his mind will allow, but he can't remember anything about a bridge. *What does she mean?*

He knows he's sleeping and probably having a dream, so he concentrates on peeling back the layers of his mind. What is she even talking about? He knows nothing of bridges . . .

And then, a tiny pinprick of a memory breaks through. Wait a minute—he remembers a pounding.

He was trying to open something. He was trying with all his might, and it still wouldn't budge. He remembers thinking *This is hopeless* as the scene plays out, hazy and indistinct.

The crushing feeling is coming back now, the dread. It's heavy and horrible, and he's stuck in an impossible situation. *What do I do now?*

He wasn't able to get her out.

I can't leave her in there.

Time was running out. He had to help her, so with every last ounce of his energy, he tried. Why did he care so much?

He scanned the area around him for something, anything he could use to open whatever it was he was trying to break. What was it? Why couldn't he remember? He didn't know what it was, he just knew that he was trying.

"Let me help you," he hears himself say out loud, wrenching him back to the present.

You can help me Kaleb, by finding Marcus.

"Who's Marcus?"

Aaron's brother.

Kaleb sighs. "I wouldn't even know where to look. And who's Aaron?"

She ignores his question. *Marcus is at the windmill. You will find him there.*

Windmill? He recalls an old property off Highway 51. There's a decrepit farmhouse there, and . . yes, a windmill.

Get help soon; they're coming.

He has so many questions. "Who's coming?"

Please, do this for me. If you can't, I know this is the end for me and Aaron. And a whole lot of other people, too.

He knows this is important, because he's feeling everything that she's feeling, but he doesn't know why. For whatever reason, he's connected to this woman.

Kaleb searches his memories for her again, trying to find where their initial connection might have occurred, but he still can't remember a thing.

Then she said something that truly baffled him. *I know there will always be good in you, Kaleb, no matter what you do or what they tell you.*

Well, that used to be true.

Forget about the contract; it doesn't matter.

How does she know about that? He never told anyone, much less her. And then he remembers the name scrolled at the bottom of those papers.

It's all a lie, Kaleb. You don't have to listen to them.

Oh, but he does. If he doesn't, he could be killed along with countless others. He doesn't have a choice now, and besides, he's quite certain that this is the same Brooke they'd warned him about. Was she tricking him? Why would she do that, and in his dream, no less?

You know what conquers all, Kaleb?

He nods. *Love.*

Just tell me where I can find you, and I will help you get out.

Find Marcus. I have to stop communicating now. They will find out I got through to you if I don't.

Kaleb found himself answering, "I will try to find this Marcus."

Thank you, Kaleb . . . and you should know something.

What's that?

I love you.

He already knows that, though he doesn't know how. But stranger still is that he finds himself answering back without even thinking about it. And the words come easily. "I love you, too."

But she's gone before she can hear them.

Kaleb wakes up feeling like something is painfully absent. He slept horribly if at all. He tossed and turned all night feeling hot as a poker one minute and shivering the next.

His sheets are damp with his sweat, and one of his limbs seems to be completely asleep and unwilling to move. He gives his body a quick once-over, and he's relieved to still have his extremities.

Well, that's something, at least.

Good grief—he needs coffee in the worst way.

He's quite sure that he dreamed of something significant last night, but for the life of him, he couldn't remember. Every couple of seconds he gets an echo and then nothing . . .

Maybe now is a good time to stop lying in bed and make something to eat. Coffee isn't going to make itself.

Maybe he's coming down with something. The flu is working its way through Neelsville, but he's feeling really hungry, and hunger and the flu don't usually go together. He wishes he'd picked up some baked goods yesterday when he had the chance.

He idly wonders if it has something to do with the contract he signed. All signs are pointing to yes. He thinks back to how the delivery driver was so peculiar and the way the papers glowed as he took them away.

Come to think of it, those papers were smoking the whole time he was holding them.

How could he have kept them in his hands if they were on fire? The man in the woods carried the same papers, and he'd noticed his demon-like claws. He shivers just thinking about it. Something wasn't right about that.

And he can't even remember his name. Wait a minute . . . yes, he does.

Mr. Black.

He feels his patience isn't what it used to be. Even though gigs are lining up quicker than anything, the most enthusiasm he can muster is a 'meh'.

This was supposed to make me happy.

He opens the kitchen window and a warm breeze filters in, caressing his face like a kiss from the sun. It's the first pleasant thing today.

I'm losing my mind.

He pours himself a cup of coffee, but in his haste, he spills some of it onto the floor. He quickly throws the mug, smashing it against the wall and showering the whole kitchen with coffee droplets. Great.

You're not losing your mind, Kaleb, you're just experiencing it at a different level, he tells himself, and he hopes he's right.

Without thinking, he grabs his keys and gets into his truck, driving toward town. He knows the bakery is open, and it's only about a seven-mile drive, so it won't be too bad. Plus, the streets aren't invaded with the Sunday crowd just yet. It's still early enough to attend a service, but he has no desire to go to church.

As he pulls up to the coffee shop, he sees a women walk out of the shop by herself, paper cup in hand, and he can't help but watch as she makes her way down the street.

He can smell her perfume and hear her chime. He likes how he can hear people now. Not them coming or going, but the music *within* them. It's like having a new sense, and as a musician, he appreciates that.

Unfamiliar feelings and urges are trying to worm their way into his brain. Societal rules and norms now seem rather pointless and silly, like he's reading them from a fairy tale.

His life is now guided by a different set of rules. They'd told him about that. They also stated that if things please him, he needn't be bothered by consequence.

Since right and wrong are thrown out the window, he almost feels like a new man. In a way, it's refreshing as hell. But being above society's rules begs the question: What kind of man is he going to be?

He parks his truck and watches as the woman in heels clicks down the sidewalk. Her hair catches the breeze, flowing like a melody in the wind. He feels a sudden urge to do things, things that his old self would not have been so proud of, and ideas burst into his brain. Like if he gets out of his truck right now, he can take her back with him to his house. *What the heck?*

What is he thinking? This isn't him—and yet, that hedonistic urge is surging through him now like a freight train. And he realizes the truth: He is more powerful now than he has ever been.

He could easily overpower her, and he won't even have to ask. *I could just put a hallucination spell on her,* he thinks. *She'd never know.*
KALEB! DON'T!

He jumps, startling at the voice in his head. *What the . . . ?* His head whips back and forth as he searches for the source. Where the hell is that coming from?

He hears her voice again. *Don't do this, Kaleb. It's not you.*

He stares at the woman as she walks away. She looks so much like Brooke . . Why is he thinking this way?

She's not me, Kaleb, and this is not you. Be strong.

He swallows hard. He needs something tangible, like a real conversation with her to believe this is real. Not some stupid back and forth in his head.

Remember the dream, Kaleb? Please remember, my friend. I am with you. These urges are just an illusion. Don't give in to them.

He's going to do it anyway. Without even thinking about it, he scans the streets to make sure no one's around, that it's just him and her. He slowly opens his door, waiting for the right moment—

Just then, a pixie-haired women pops up beside his truck.

"Hiya."

The woman looks him up and down, appraising him, and he shifts under her scrutiny.

"Looks like we arrived in time."

Kaleb blinks at her audacity. "In time for what?"

Before he can even get a foot out of his truck, he feels a zap on his shoulder. Everything goes black.

$$\text{\Moon}$$

Avery

Kaleb slumps over in his seat, and Avery shoves him as Iris climbs in the passenger side. "Slide him over so I can drive, please."

"Gladly."

"Oh, look! He's a cutie." Iris giggles beside her.

"Iris, we're on a mission. Can you behave?"

"Shut up. Do you even know how to drive a truck?"

"Please, how hard can it be?" The gears grind as she tries to get the vehicle to start, and Iris rolls her eyes from beside her. Avery decides it will be better to recite a chant. "Start up right now before I put you out of commission."

The truck turns on with ease.

"I think the next thing is shifting it into 1st."

Avery shoots her an angry glare. "That's fine, Iris, I got it from here."

"Wonderful. Where to?"

She nods at the unconscious being between them. "We need to take this creature back to his home; we can ask him questions there. Then we'll attempt a reversal of this disease, if that's even still possible."

"Is it too late?"

"If he's newly infected, there's always a chance."

"Then what?"

"Then, we need to find Marcus."

THE VISITORS

The Traveller

I spend a good portion of my evenings reflecting on my long life. I do this while sitting on my dock. I like being near water, and fishing makes me happy, too—it all makes me feel like a better version of myself, however temporary.

Right now, I'm watching the sun set itself into the lake. I've seen this thousands of times, and I never tire of it.

Acute vibrations sing through the air tonight, it sounds similar to what I heard on that dreadful boat ride. As I scan the surface of the lake, I am puzzled. I see two heads pop up out of the middle of it. I'm not expecting visitors, but I'm not exactly surprised, either.

They look like they are both female. I watch as they swim in unison down the middle of the lake, making their way closer to me.

Two supernaturals at the same time? I smell a trickery.

They're headed straight for my dock. As I wait for them to arrive, I notice the wildlife has fallen silent. This means one of two things: There is a predator in the area, or these women are supernatural beings. Animals can sense something amiss, and they protect themselves by staying silent and hiding. They don't do this with me—they know what I am, how I walk the earth, so they consider me rather harmless.

I run into other supernatural beings from time to time, and there is always a mutual understanding. We don't bother each other; the last thing either of us wants to do is make any kind of scene. We do our mutual best to blend in with the human population. And besides, I hate social situations anyway.

But I don't care for these ad hoc kind of meetings. I prefer preparation; I'm no good at spur of the moment. That's more Penny's area of expertise.

Most of my conversations are with her anyway. Sometimes in conversation I am not even aware of the year I am in. Even the time of day sometimes alludes me. I'm awkward, so I know my manners are not up to par. Things change so drastically over the decades, and I never know what is truly appropriate for right now, I've stopped paying attention. And to be honest, I tend to forget.

But since I know they've both seen me, I can't leave. They're headed right this way, swimming in a ghostly fashion. *Well, this ought to be fun.*

I watch them closely. If they try something rash, I will kill them. Penny is my highest priority, and I will protect her at all costs.

They emerge from the lake in unison, standing there in front of me in their dripping wet clothes. I stand up, I want them to see me, look me over. They stare at me, and I glance back and forth between them.

After a moment of silence, I break out the pleasantries.

"So, what brings you ladies to Neelsville this fine evening?"

"Oh God, really?" the one with the strange hair asks.

"Shut your mouth, Iris."

One of them is salty. Noted.

"Good evening, sir. I'm Avery, and little Miss Prickly Pants here is my sister, Iris."

"Glad to meet you."

"And your name, sir?"

I might as well just speak it out.

"They call me, the Traveller."

"Okay, Mr. Traveller."

The nicer of the two--*Avery*--seems to be the one in charge.

"We are here on business," she says.

"Business of what kind?"

"The family kind. We're looking for our brother, Marcus."

Iris chimes in. "We have reason to believe that he's been taken against his will. And were quite sure they've captured our other brother, Aaron."

I scan both of them, searching their minds. I feel that they are not here for harm; just in need of answers.

Iris continues. "You know this town is almost infected?"

"I'm well aware of the state of this town."

Avery shakes her head. "You'll have to excuse my sister, Iris. She's not what they call 'socially competent.'"

Iris rolls her eyes.

"Well, then we have something in common—neither am I."

A tiny smile spreads across Avery's face. "So you're okay with what is going on around here?"

"That wouldn't be very prudent of me, would it?"

"Not that we care; we don't live here."

"Iris!" Avery hisses.

Iris ignores her. "Listen, Traveller; we want to help the humans living here. One of our brothers has already succumbed."

"And we still need to find Marcus." Avery adds.

The salty girl scoffs. "Every time they spend time with this Brooke, they end up missing."

"It's not her fault, Iris!"

Iris rolls her eyes again. "Listen, Traveller, we know of your powers. If you can help us in any way, we will be forever grateful." She spares a glance at her sister who's glaring in her general direction. "We also have a new distractor. He's out cold, for now. Could you possibly help us with him?"

They want my help? They must be joking.

"I don't intervene in things unless I absolutely have to."

I don't mention the situation at the gas station the other day.

Avery turns to him. "We think you can help this lost soul. Would you help us?"

I let out a huge sigh.

All I wanted this evening was a little bit of rest. And yet, here I am, getting pulled into other problems.

I hear Penny as she calls down to the group. She is in our cabin, and probably enjoying a good book. "I've put on a pot of tea, honey—why don't you invite our guests in? I would love to meet them."

God bless my Penny. She must have heard the conversation—heck, she probably even saw them coming.

"Tea would be great; thank you," Iris ventures.

"Wonderful. We have things to discuss."

Well, I guess there is no stopping it. I lead both of them up to the ivy-lined steps to our cabin.

"Beautiful place you have here," Avery offers.

"We like it."

The salty one—Iris--can't seem to be bothered by walking up stairs. I watch as she snaps her fingers and immediately floats up to the top.

"Oh, Iris!" Avery calls.

"You know I don't care for steps!" She yells back.

"You'll have to excuse Iris," Avery speaks. "Being decent is a stretch for her. She's even worse with the humans."

I chuckle and agree. "I can only imagine."

Once we reach the top of the stairs, I lead them to our cabin and through the front door.

Penny welcomes them with her smile, and sweet demeanor.

"I made cinnamon tea. I don't know what you both like, but it's a favorite of mine."

God, I love her.

"That will be perfect, thank you," Avery says, a genial smile on her face.

I feel the need to jump in with the introductions. "Penny, this is Avery and Iris."

"Well, how do you do?" Penny asks the two women. "I can see you came from far away."

Iris laughs. "Sure."

I watch as Avery and Iris scan their surroundings before finding a seat at our round wooden coffee table. Penny has fixed a tray of fancy cookies sitting in the middle, and Iris reaches for one as Avery shoots her a look.

I watch as Avery glances out our huge picture window overlooking the lake. She seems to like what she sees. Penny has done a good job with making our house into a home.

Avery begins to speak. "There are things going on here that just aren't natural."

I couldn't agree with you more.

"I agree."

"We can intervene," Iris offers. "Do you feel the humans here are worth saving?"

"There are lots of people worth saving here," Penny notes, catching Iris's gaze and holding it. Iris is the one to finally look away.

My eyes are tuned into Avery—there is something about her—wait a minute!!

I know her. But, from where?

I scan through my vast amount of memories to quickly try and recall. I then freeze in my thoughts. She notices that I might have remembered something about her.

"You were there, weren't you? You were the one helping." She says.

And I can barely utter the words.

"Yes, the bridge."

She nods, and a large smile crosses her face. "You're the one they talk about. The Traveller."

"Who talks of me?"

"Only everyone. Our kind has heard the rumors for years. Tales of the great one that likes to roam the corners of the earth, trying to help the humans."

"I wouldn't say 'likes.'"

"What happened to you?" Iris asks.

What happened to me? Now there's a question.

"I'm not at liberty to discuss it. I've come to terms with my own existence, though, and I wouldn't say it was a choice."

I glance over at Penny, and smile.

"My life has been considerably better the last twenty years—that I'm sure of."

Iris pipes up. "The accident at the bridge killed many humans."

"Yes, it did. And I will eternally regret that I did not do more."

Avery's face softens. "You did plenty. I didn't see anyone else helping."

"You helped."

She nods, swallowing once. "We tried, but as you know, there was only so much we could do." Her eyes are sad. "Did they ever invite you to their meetings?"

I think back to those wretched, god-forsaken meetings. I don't care to admit, but I best be truthful if I want these women on my side.

"I attended a few of them. So I knew what was going to happen, which makes me an accessory."

"But you helped those people!" Penny yells.

I didn't feel like I really helped anybody.

"I helped very little, dear."

Avery pipes up. "I saw you helping, Traveller. Several people took notice when we all joined in to help. But the whole situation, as you know, was hopeless."

"I never felt right after those meetings; I stopped going after the third one. I shouldn't have associated with those beings. They're bad news, to say the least."

I think back to that awful day. Another event that I can recall like it was yesterday. Somewhere near dusk on a temperate December evening, the bridge had collapsed, taking the cars lining its deck down with it. I remember how they looked all floating towards the bottom of the lake, headlights on, and engines still running.

I remember the screams.

"We tried to help," Iris jumps in, "but as you know, they maximized the destruction. They certainly pulled off an elaborate scheme—they must have planned that for months in advance."

"They most certainly did." I say.

Avery leans forward. "So how do we stop them?"

"There is no stopping them. They're like squirrely little varmints weaving their way into crevices, wreaking havoc wherever they can."

And their powers have no boundaries.

She considers my statement.

"That is true. I've come across a few myself. Can't say that I like them much." Avery says.

Her sister interjects. "Do you always play by the rules?"

I glare at Iris's retort. But I really can't blame her—it's a fair question—but she is overstepping herself here. And there is no need to start an argument. I decide to shift gears. "Can't say I'm much for the travelling anymore. From now on, I will be staying in place, letting the cards fall where they may."

"I'm sorry." Avery's words are soft.

I look over at my wife, and reach for her hand. "Don't be. I met Penny, my true mate in life. Only took two thousand years, but she was well worth the wait."

Penny leans over and gives me a kiss.

"Where did you guys meet?" Avery asks.

I take in a breath. "We met because of the bridge."

"Um, hello?" Iris's shrill voice would've hurt my ears had I still been human.

I know what she's getting at. She stares at my dear Penny, her eyes narrowing in her assessment. "How is she possible?"

"It's none of your business," I shoot back, "but since you're so curious, she's well preserved."

Penny stands and reaches for the tray, leaning in for another kiss before heading back into the kitchen.

"Preserved?" Avery asks. "You can do that?"

"Most certainly. It's the one allowance I was given: I stopped her aging."

Avery looks around, a bit amused.

"But what about her parents, her family? Aren't they gonna know?"

"Don't you think I've taken that into account? She has no family to speak of. Her mom passed away years ago. Her father, well, he left her family."

"He just left?" Iris blinks.

"No one can find him. Besides, he would be very old, if not dead, by now anyway."

Penny comes back into the room and sets another tray of snacks down on the table. "Sometimes bad things happen to allow other things to fall into place. Not that I care for bad things; it's just the way of it sometimes." She smirks. "And besides, I certainly don't mind looking so young."

I would do anything for my dear Penny.

"Penny knew about the bridge weeks beforehand, and she's human." I say.

Iris cocks her head to one side, scanning me up and down. I know she disapproves.

"If you can get rid of these things, why don't you?"

"I'm not meant to intervene."

I watch then as Penny takes a sip of her tea and stares at our wall full of books. Given the way she's sitting and the odd slant of her wrist, I know what's coming next: she's about to have one of her visions.

Her visions are always informative, but they always end up wearing her out. She'll probably be in bed for days afterward, but that's okay. I will be there to take care of her, as I always do.

She sets down her cup of tea and stares up at the ceiling. She starts to raise her hands in the air and closes her eyes.

"What," Iris starts, "may I ask, is she doing?"

"She's having a vision."

The young woman swallows hard. "Oh."

Avery chimes in. "Does she get these a lot?"

"Quite often, yes. They are pretty spot-on, though, so I wouldn't interfere.

I scan the space in front of my mate.

"Avery, would you mind moving those out of the way?" I point to a couple of easy chairs next to where we are all sitting.

Avery scrambles to move the furniture out of the way as Penny lifts off the couch and starts dancing in a circle. She moves slowly at first, her eyes closed, her arms extended out at her sides.

"She's coming," she breathes, "A future mate is coming. She will be at the door soon."

"How did a human acquire such advances?" Avery whispers to me.

"How does anyone acquire anything? But I am more than fine with it."

We watch as Penny twirls about the room, clearly overcome with emotion. It is such a beautiful thing to behold, and I am mesmerized by her. She begins to speak.

"There are gross injustices here; they're all around us. You need to find your brother. He's at the windmill. He's there right now."

"He's at the windmill?" Iris perks up.

"There's a windmill not far from here, Iris," Penny answers, her eyes still closed, her hands high in the air.

"What are we waiting for?" Iris moves to stand, but Avery's hand grips her arm, holding her in place. Iris glares at her sister.

Penny continues. "They captured Aaron."

"Where is he?!" Iris screams.

"He's far away."

Iris huffs. "I knew it. I can't stand her."

"Brooke is there, too," Penny asserts, somehow understanding who "her" is. "She's still in their pools, replicating."

Avery gasps. "What?!"

"They took her yesterday evening."

"Who took her, Penny?" I ask.

"The doctor. The one at the med center. Though he's not a doctor anymore, the human side of him is gone." Penny keeps dancing. "You need to get the singer before he fully turns."

Then she starts laughing hysterically. "Your future mate is coming; she will be at the door in five minutes."

"Future mate? What is she talking about?" Avery asks, finding my gaze.

"She gets tired sometimes, especially towards the end, it starts to sound like gibberish."

I turn to Penny. "It's okay, honey. You can come out of it now."

She collapses then, and I scoop her up before she hits the ground, laying her down on the couch.

"Can we help with anything?" Avery asks.

"Maybe a cold cloth. These visions tend to make her run a temperature."

"Sure." Avery scans the room.

"Really, sis? We can just manifest it, you know." Iris says.

Iris soon produces a chilly washcloth and gives it to Avery to put on Penny's neck. "Is the vision done?"

Her vision seemed to be done, but this one looked like it took its toll.

"Let's give her some room." I say.

Just then, there's a knock at the door. Avery looks over at me and raises an eyebrow. "Expecting visitors?"

What now?

"It's not often we have guests." I say.

I steel myself with a deep breath, and wonder why I am having so many guests in one day. I open the door and stare at the strange female standing before me. Her arms are folded across her chest, and she looks angry.

I don't know of this nonsense, and I'm not sure how to talk to her. But just by the way she is standing, I can tell she is of a different sort.

"They call me Scout." She glances past me into the room.

"And would you all mind telling me what the hell is going on around here?"

THE CAR RIDE

The Traveller

I just stare at her as she pushes her way into the room.
Who is this young beast, and what is she talking about?
"I know weird things are going on around here. I just saw
two heads come up out of the middle of the lake." She glares at the
women on either side of me. Penny is still lying on the couch. She
continues on.

"Unless you two got lungs for days, I don't see how that's possible.
I think you'd all better explain to me what is going on around here."

I watch as her hip juts out, demanding an explanation. She looks
like a handful of trouble. God help any man who tries to tame her.

Iris stands across from Scout and gives her a dirty look. "We don't
need to explain anything to you, little human."

"Let her speak, Iris," Avery admonishes.

Scout straightens. "I know you're sisters of Aaron and Marcus, and
I happen to be a friend of Brooke's. You know, Brooke? She's gone
now, too, and I'm scared. She told me about Penny and your cabin

up here, and I feel like this is the only safe place to be right now. I wouldn't be here otherwise."

As I hear her words, I can't help but start to feel for her. She continues on.

"You have to believe me. I had a creepy-ass dream the other night involving a resident here, you know, the one that was murdered last year. She lives close by Brooke's place, just off Pony Road."

"We believe you, Scout," I finally tell her.

She looks over and keeps going. "And here's the thing. Some tall, creepy, man is slithering around my aunt's house, asking for her in the middle of the night. Who the hell does that?"

"Distractors," Penny says from the couch as she pushes up to sitting.

Scout glances her way before turning back to me. "Well, whatever they are, they make me want to drag my ass back down to Florida. You know how bad it has to be for me to want to do that?"

"Bad?" I offer. I can't help but find the humor in it, there is something funny about her. She looks my way and doesn't hesitate.

"Aren't you an Einstein, well, yeah."

I grin back.

"Okay, back up," Iris jumps in. "When did you realize that Brooke is gone?"

"Last night. She was babysitting at some farmhouse around here, but she never came home. No one seems to be home over at her house. Not her parents, her sister, anyone."

Penny's eyes grow wide. "They took her."

"Avery, we need to get to Marcus," Iris says.

"Yes, we do." Avery nods then turns to Scout. "Listen, do you know where the windmill is around here?"

"Everyone knows."

"Can you take us there? We need to find our brother."

Scout shrugs. "Sure. How are we getting there?"

I didn't want to get involved, but it would appear that this will be the case. I offer my help.

"We can take our car," I say.

Avery pushes to her feet. "We also have the singer, he's infected but we might be able to help him. He's asleep at his place."

I nod. "First things first."

"I want to come, too!" Penny chimes in from the couch.

I glance her way. I feel like she should rest on the couch.

"Honey, I think you should stay here and rest."

She gives me a strong scowl. "Rest? I don't want to rest! Besides, I'd like to see this windmill. I want to see it up close."

"Okay," I concede. "But I would feel better if you stayed in the car."

"We wouldn't let any of them get to her anyway." Iris calls from where she and Avery are putting the last of their dishes in the kitchen sink.

"Well, I appreciate that, Iris."

Hmm, maybe I'm starting to win the salty one over. I shoot her a grateful glance as we all step outside. We cross the lawn, head into the garage and pile into our van. I appraise each of them as they get in.

What a motley group.

"I have to say, driving isn't exactly my strong suit."

Penny pats my leg, she's trying to reassure me. "I can drive if you want, dear."

She is in no condition to drive, so I get in the driver's seat.

"Let's just get there already," I say.

As I back out of the drive, I start to get one on my itchy feelings. Maybe it's coming from the windmill. Or maybe it's from all this activity. Like I said, having visitors is not common for us.

"We need to get there before they take Marcus," Penny says, her voice strained.

"And then we need to get the singer," Avery adds.

I nod, my gaze fixed on the road. I'm going a little faster than what I usually prefer, but the roads here are usually clear this time of the evening. The town itself isn't all that populated, which helps.

I can sense the urgency in the air. Especially from Iris.

"We need to get to him, Avery. You know what they'll do if they find him first."

Avery sighs at her sister. "We're going, Iris; be patient."

Up ahead, I have about two seconds before I see a young fawn dart out right in front of my car. I yank at the wheel, veering back and forth. I'm swerving all over the road.

I'm losing control of this car.

"Everyone, hang on!" I yell.

Iris screams from the backseat.

"Where the hell did you get your license?" Scout yells from beside her.

I ignore everyone.

Get control of this van.

"Hang on!" I yell.

"Do a spell, Avery; get us back on the road!!" Iris shouts.

Avery's yelling, too. "You know it doesn't work like that! I would have had to do it beforehand."

I'm trying my best, I really am. But there is no stopping a tree, and we're headed right for it. In the next moment, the trunk of this massive oak is filling the windshield.

That's the last thing I remember, before everything goes dark.

☽

I am vaguely aware that the side of my face is lying on the road. The jagged pavement is cutting into my cheek, and this is what stirs me awake. This feeling of not wanting to move is foreign to me. Several bones in my body feel broken, but I know this sensation is temporary. I'll be back to one-hundred percent in about an hour. For whatever that's worth.

As I look around from the standpoint of the ground, I wonder how I could have strayed so far from the accident—I must have been thrown from the car. It's odd that I can't remember. This is not something I am used to.

Why did I have to drive so damn fast?

My thoughts are interrupted by a shout. "Traveller!"

It is Avery, and her voice hits me in the chest like a gong. I try and make my way to sitting, and as I do, panic surges through me.

Where is she? Where's my Penny?

I look around and see a mangled version of the car, it rests a few feet back. I scramble to my feet and sprint towards it, the memory of the crash coming back in a rush. I can see Scout crawling out the back window.

"Are you okay?"

"I'm fine," she says. But waves me off as she struggles to get herself upright, then falls back to the ground. I look around, desperate. "Where is Penny?" I yell.

Please be alive.

I walk around to the side of the car, bracing myself for what I might see. Right away I see Penny's head sticking out from the hood of it, her body halfway through the windshield.

Oh my God!

I try and pick out the glass, but it's everywhere. It makes her whole body shimmer in the light.

"Call an ambulance!" Avery shouts from where she is standing. I shake my head.

"Well, isn't that what you guys do here?" she retorts, running to my side.

I stare at her blankly. "This is an accident. You know a human can't handle this kind of beating."

I gaze down at my Penny, She's slumped over in my arms and already starting to look like a deflated version of herself. She won't be with us much longer, I know this in my being. I pull her closer, I want to feel her lovely warmth. I wrap my arms arounds her to keep it between us, and I whisper in her ear. "Penny my love, please stay with us."

Avery is standing by my side. She places a gentle hand on my shoulder. "What can I do?"

I ignore her question as I hold Penny's body in my arms. "I can do a rejuvenation spell," she offers. "Spells can heal her, I've seen it a bunch of times."

"Spells are not going to work now!" I utter.

I let my words resonate, and I can tell she is perplexed, having no idea what to do next.

Scout is still sitting in the road. I notice Iris--who was watching Penny's demise from several feet away—push to her feet.

"I'll go help Scout."

I hear Scout moaning, as Iris asks where is hurts.

"Everywhere. I think I'm gonna die."

"You're not going to die."

Scout calls out, and I guess she's trying to get up. "But I can't move anything!," she cries.

"Just sit still." I hear the growing irritation in Iris's voice. "Just shut-up, I'm going to heal you."

"What the hell can't you guys do?"

"Quiet, please," Iris snipes back. "I need to concentrate."

I watch as Scout closes her eyes, lying still as Iris trails her hands over her entire body. I know it's working, I can see it float out of her and into the air. It's a strange vapor swirling around us, I watch as it fades into nothingness. Scout will be ok.

I turn my attention back to the only women that I have ever loved. My lover, my soulmate, my everything. I'm alarmed at how much she has deteriorated in the few minutes that I'd looked away. In the background I can hear Scout talking to Iris.

"What can we do?"

"I don't think there's anything we can do, Scout. Remember the preservation thing he put on her?"

I don't hear her response, and I feel myself turning numb.

"When he did that, he took away any second chance for her. A healing spell is not going to work. He's probably realizing this right now."

Well, aren't you just the brightest bulb in the package.

Her words ring harsh in the air, but they are true, and I need to hear it.

This is all my fault.

Scout offers a one-word response. "Crap."

I am aware that my heart might not make it through this. I can feel it trying to tear in two, as my love prepares to leave this world. "Oh, my dear Penny."

"It's not anyone's fault." I hear Avery say. But her voice catches then. She sees something ahead of us. I follow her gaze just in time to see that God forsaken fawn. We all watch as it shape-shifts back into the distractor it is, as it turns to run off into the woods. I snarl at it.

"I should have figured it was one of them." She curses. "I'm gonna go after it."

"Don't," Iris commands as she walks up, Scout at her side. "We still need to find Marcus, then get to the singer. I need you here. Although now I don't know when it's appropriate to leave." I can feel the cold stares of everyone around me. I wish they would leave me be. I don't care what they do.

I want to be alone with her.

"Go find Marcus, Iris," Avery says. "Just follow your instincts. You're close enough now to find the windmill. I'll stay with them."

"What about Scout?"

I tune out of their conversation and turn back to my wife. As I watch her, a fresh wave of sorrow washes over me. "Dear, oh sweet dear. I'm so sorry."

Her eyes blink open, as she catches my gaze. I watch, helpless, as she struggles to draw in breath. "Don't be sorry," she rasps. "We had a lot of fun together, didn't we?"

Subtle changes are happening right before my eyes, and I am powerless to stop it. This is what kills me. With every passing minute, Penny is dying. The preservation spell has completely worn off, it won't be long now.

I keep her close. Just about everything is covered in her blood. Her face is now etched in wrinkles, her chestnut hair turning grey, and yet, she's never been more beautiful.

I take one last look at my love, and with her final breath, she dies in my arms.

A NEW PATH

The Traveller

*I*t's the middle of the night, I think. I'm not sure because I've lost all track of time. But as I walk, I hear the bullfrogs, they croak on during this hideous night. And the moon casts its shadow upon me. I can smell jasmine in the night breeze floating throughout the trees.

I'm holding Penny's lifeless body in my arms, and time no longer exists for me. Her blood has started soaking into my clothing.

I don't think I'll ever want to shower again—I want her blood on me forever. I want to remember every single piece of her. Even the tangy smell of it smeared across my arms, my face, wherever her body has touched mine, I want to commit it to memory. All of these things I cannot let go.

I will never let go.

I carry her to the part of the woods where we always enjoyed walking. Deep in the heart of it, there's a grove of lilac bushes right in the middle of all the wildflowers and weeds. I don't know why they're growing there; someone must have planted them years before. They are fragrant in early summer—Penny would often pick handfuls of it and place them in a vase in our cabin. And our home would smell like heaven, just like her.

This is where I will bury her.

With each shovelful of dirt, I feel my humanity start to fall away. Well, perhaps that happened long ago, and I didn't know it. But I feel it now—I feel it getting weaker with each dig in the dirt.

There's an odd peace to that, not giving a shit about anything. The deeper I dig, the wider the chasm in my heart grows. I know I'm coming unglued. I feel lunacy trying to take hold, and for once, I'm going to let it.

These supernaturals and the human had better stay clear of me because I have an itching urge to kill them all. That's what I want to do. I can't think of a reason to try and be good anymore.

Because there isn't any.

I feel one of them sit down next to me. Her small voice asking me silly questions. Like I care about anything she says. I can barely hear her over the constant ringing in my ears. Because of who I am, every part of me that's broken will be knitted back to health within the hour, so the ringing—and the searing pain all over my body—will soon go away. I wish it wouldn't, *I want to suffer.*

They want to make it right, placate me. But nothing about this is right, and it never will be.

"Traveller?"

I stare straight ahead.

"I'm sorry to bother you."

But you are. It's the supernatural again, the one in charge. I don't want to acknowledge her, but she's insisting that I do. She's like a barking hound that never shuts up.

"What would you like us to do?" Avery says.

He ponders this. What can anybody do? "You can start by keeping the human away from me."

"You mean Scout?"

"Yes, I mean Scout. There are things about her that remind me of Penny. I can't have that around me right now. Keep her clear of me, you understand?"

"I do." Avery sighs. "Traveller, this is not your fault."

"Yeah, right."

I should have known better. I was driving too fast, and this was very much my fault.

Avery

Avery watches the Traveller cover his face with his hands as he sits down on the ground, as Penny's lifeless body lies next to him. It's a sad thing to witness, and she wants to lay her hands on him, but she doesn't dare.

The Traveller suddenly uncovers his face, swipes roughly at the tears on his cheeks, and produces a shovel she only now realizes he grabbed from the trunk of his car. As he plunges the tool in the ground, Avery notices that the accident had accelerated Penny's aging process. While he digs, her body takes on the appearance of a haggard old woman. She's a different sight entirely and looks nothing like she did before. Avery's gut clenches and her eyes widen as she takes in the now dried-up, white-haired shell of Penny's former self.

Life can be so cruel.

She looks decades older than she did just a few hours ago when she was making tea for everyone back at the cabin. Penny, with her delicate hands and long fingers, is no more.

She can't bear to look at her.

Avery doesn't care for this violent, chaotic world called Earth and will be happy to leave once things are back to normal. But right now, she's wondering if it will ever be normal again. Or if it ever was.

The Traveller tosses the shovel on the grass, and Avery blinks at the impressive grave he's excavated in such a short amount of time. He's strong, or he was. She's afraid of what this will do to him.

"I'm sorry, but shouldn't you be calling the authorities?" she asks. "You want to report this, don't you?"

He glares at her.

"Sorry, I just don't know what the proper protocol is here."

"No one is calling anyone. Look at her! How the hell would I explain that? You know how the humans are with all their annoying questions, I will do nothing of the sort. Go back to my cabin; it's yours now."

"What?"

"I'm not coming back, not ever."

"What do you mean? Let me help you," Avery pleads.

"I don't want your help. Don't you understand?" he screams, and Avery takes a step back.

"But what will you do?" she ventures. "Where will you go?"

He grunts. "Just leave me be, and go find your brother."

She doesn't move.

"Just leave, now!"

The tone of his voice has her hurrying away. Avery finds Scout and Iris back at the accident scene and tells them what happened. She takes

Scout back to the cabin, telling her to wait there. Once that's done, Iris helps her roll the van off the road and into the woods so nothing can be seen—she doubts anyone will be looking for it anyway, but if they start, it will take some digging.

GETTING CLOSER

Mr. Sardine

*M*r. Sardine finds the house, easy peasy. He steps out of his van with an extra pep in his step. He catches a glimpse of his reflection in the rearview, but this time, he can't help but grin.

He admires the reflection staring back at him, and that's never happened before. Gone were the pockmarks, the shifty eyes, the lack of confidence.

Today, his skin is flawless, his eyes sparkle with wisdom, and there's a surge of confidence that he hasn't felt before.

So, this is what it's like to feel good in your own skin.

If this is what it means to be a distractor, he should have done it long ago. This is so much better than living life as a mere human—just having this inner awareness now—it's incomparable.

He never liked the way he looked before, ever. And after this last set of papers is delivered, he'll be one step closer to his goal of being one-hundred percent distractor. He's finally down to less than fifty stops, and then his initial work will be complete.

The higher-ups have promised him a good stretch of land—several acres—in Mexico. It's such a sweet deal that he's having trouble believing this is his new reality. Butterflies are constantly floating in his stomach—he can't imagine having all that property attached to his name. And hanging with all the superior distractors down there in Mexico will be a nice perk.

He's heard that all of their vacation homes are the size of summer resorts, i.e. *dripping with money.* Sardine finds that ironic since he remembers his earlier onversations with Avalone on that very topic. In fact, he recalls him completely dismissing the notion of it, even going so far as to say, *"Money doesn't exist in our organization."*

The comment had given him pause, but it's possible he could have just heard him wrong. But how could anyone acquire such vast amounts of property and wealth without money?

Regardless, Mexico is one big distractor party, and he wants in on it.

Their inner workings fascinate him. He always likes it when they ask him to deliver something special to their meetings like flowers or certain refreshments. He is never allowed to stay, of course; that permission only granted once he becomes a full distractor. But sometimes he will catch bits and pieces of idle conversations, like how they want to do something and what city they want to do it in, and he wishes he could stay as a fly on the wall. It's all one giant game, and soon he will play a part in it. Especially once his new company, Use Industries, gets off the ground.

Evening stops aren't all that unusual for Sardine, but the previous one took him longer than anticipated. The signer had been balking at his contract, and Sardine had to roll out the red carpet, so to speak. He will mention that to the higher-ups; maybe they'll give him a bonus.

AN AWAKENING

The steps leading up to the walkway of this house are round and uneven and made up of mostly stones. He recognizes these stones— they're agates—and for a brief moment, he's taken back to long after- noons of agate hunting with his grandfather. He used to love doing that with him during his summers in Duluth. Seems like a lifetime ago.

He can't believe he almost forgot about it.

Now, the memory seems bittersweet, almost too painful to remem- ber. He turns his attention to the ivy covering up the steps in a pleas- ant, homey way.

He likes these people already.

All he had been told about this stop is that the wife is one-hun- dred percent on board, but the husband, not so much. He needs to be prepared in case things take a turn for the worse. But that was okay. Sometimes spouses need extra convincing for this sort of thing. He likes to look at it like a married couple practicing two different reli- gions—as long as they can convert one of them, it's considered a win.

Sardine's latent distractor traits are finally starting to flourish. If things were to take a dicey turn, he could conjure up a full-blown distractor in a few minutes' time. It's hard to comprehend having this kind of power, but he supposes he'll just have to get used to it.

Standing outside the screen door on their porch, he hears the begin- nings of her chime before he even lays eyes on her, and it's heaven to his ears. He closes his eyes and smiles—it almost feels like coming home. There's a sensual quality to it that makes him catch his breath. He so likes this new ability, hearing the musical melody of humans.

As she comes into view, he first thinks he's looking at an angel. When she opens the door, he smells the sweet notes of her perfume, such a stark contrast to the forest, and he's reminded of his mother. She used to wear the same kind.

Long-dormant feelings and urges stir inside him. She greets him with a warm smile, and the gesture draws his attention to the stark red of her lipstick.

Did she put that on for me? God, I hope so. The thought makes him blush.

He's always appreciated women who take care of themselves, even though he was often ignored by them. As a human, feelings of unworthiness covered him like a lifelong malaise, a continual pain that gnawed at him daily. And over the years, he came to accept this reality.

But now, with his upgraded looks and sense of purpose, he's exhilarated by the notion of catching the eye of an attractive women. She winks at him, motioning for him to sit down at the kitchen table.

"Sit over here, doll." She says, as she gives him a once-over.

"You look like you could use a drink."

He finds her commanding quality pleasing. Sardine could always use a drink, but he doesn't like to drink with his clients. Drinking tends to make them sloppy, and he can't afford to have that sloppiness find its way to him.

However, for her, he would make an exception. "Sure, thank you."

As she mixes his drink, the husband walks into the room and extends his hand. Sardine returns his firm handshake and notes the resolute look in his eye.

This guy is no-nonsense, which indicates the potential for danger.

Sardine reminds himself about his abilities. *He* is the one with the advantage here, and back-up is always available. He just wishes he could get a better read on him.

Her voice breaks into his thoughts. "Oh, Christ!"

The tone in her chime has gone up several octaves, and a scowl mars her pretty face.

He watches as she holds a large bottle of Jack Daniels under her nose, and takes a sip.

"Ma'am?"

"I knew it!" she yells.

"What?" Sardine asks. "I knew it! Someone's been messing around with my booze."

Sardine glances over as the man rolls his eyes. "What are you talking about?"

"It's been watered down, Lyles!

"Now who would water down perfectly good booze?"

"You know exactly who. Scout!"

"Damn shitshow around here," Lyle whispers under his breath.

"I'm gonna tar and feather that girl. Why would she go and do a thing like that?"

The man sighs. "I wouldn't know, Cassie."

Sardine can feel Cassie's anger percolating inside her, and he starts to see patches of red across her neck and chest.

She glares at Lyle. "By the way, why aren't you mad? Whiskey isn't exactly cheap, you know."

"I pick my battles with you, Cassie; you know that. I swear I'm gonna die of a heart attack one day, and you're gonna be the one to do it!"

Cassie bypasses his statement. "When Scout gets back here, she'll have lots of explaining to do."

"I'll have a talk with her."

Sardine shifts in his seat. Is it hot in here? "Maybe I should go," he suggests.

Cassie lights up a cigarette as her eyes scan him head to toe. "You'll do nothing of the sort. Make yourself comfortable. I won't be long; the liquor store is just down the road."

Sardine's eyes flit around the room, and Cassie seems to notice. "Oh, don't worry about Lyles; he wouldn't swat a fly."

Sardine has his doubts.

"Say, do you happen to like hot nuts?"

Sardine just stares at her.

"I made a batch of them yesterday," she says as she pulls a can out and flips off the lid, setting it on the table. "Turned out just perfect—I finally managed to get the right amount of cayenne in this batch. Help yourself."

With every passing moment, her presence is making him feel lighter. She's a high that won't go away.

She gives him another wink. "I'll be back before you've even had a chance to lick all your fingers."

She hands Sardine the can of nuts and lets herself out. Sardine glances over at Lyle, who is clearly amused.

"Better listen to her, fella, I'd grab yourself a seat."

Sardine sits down at the table, pops a handful in his mouth, and tries his best to remain patient until Cassie's return. He has fingers he wants to lick, all right, but they sure aren't his.

THE PHONE CALL

Margie

*M*argie is on edge. Various creatures have been coming out of the woodwork lately like the cockroaches they are, and she doesn't know what to do about it.

She jumps about three feet in the air when her coral colored phone rings. As she gets closer to it, she notices large, oily splotches that seem to be everywhere.

Crap, these walls do need a good scrubbing down.

The phone rings again, and she wants to rip it off the wall.

One of the patrons at the bar glances over. "You gonna answer that, Marge?"

That's the last thing she wants to do. She knows it's Mavis, and if she's calling, it only means trouble.

She closes her eyes, picks up the phone, and braces herself.

"What took you so long?"

And just like that, all past arguments with Mavis come rushing to the surface. "Oh, I don't know, Mavis; maybe I have a business to run."

"What if I was a customer wanting to order some lunch? Maybe you should hop to it, start treating your bar like the business it is."

Mavis could always be nasty, that part of her hasn't changed. Margie could feel all the joy of her day starting to ooze out of her. "What do you want, Mavis?"

"Well, you'll appreciate this call because I have bigger fish to fry than our sibling spat. One of them strange things is headed your way. And by my calculations, they should be there in the next few minutes."

"What?" Margie hisses into the phone. She so doesn't want to deal with this right now.

"Yes. Now pay attention to this, Margie; I'm serious. You need to know what they can do."

"I'm well aware of what they're capable of, Mavis."

"I really don't know if you do, Margie—so please listen! They have these markings, okay? Especially the newly minted ones. It's right at the back of their neck, so be on the lookout for it. And if you need to buy some time, find yourself some table salt. You can pour it around you like a barrier. They won't cross over it as long as it's there."

"Table salt? How do you know this stuff?"

"Don't ask me—I don't make the damn rules. Now get to it before it gets there."

"Do you know who it is?"

"Listen, you want me pouring the salt for you, too? You don't have this kind of time. Whatever it is, it's not of this earth. Just get it out of your bar, okay? Keep it short and sweet, and don't act all weird."

"I'm not going to act weird, Mavis—you have that whole department covered."

Mavis's laughter echoes through the phone. Margie yanks it away from her ear for a second, wincing. "I'm so glad you're finding this humorous."

"You wouldn't believe the things I find funny. Now go!"

Mavis hangs up the phone, leaving Margie standing there, wondering where she last put her saltshakers.

Think.

First things first. She'll first need to get her dogs, Adam and Eve, out the back door. She doesn't want them getting killed.

She scans her bar, noticing there are still a good amount of people here. She doesn't want to cause a scene with everyone so close.

Find the salt.

She dashes behind the bar, frantically throwing things around in her search for the shakers but having no luck. The bell above the door rings, announcing her next customer. She peers over the bar, and of course, it's her dear friend, Cassie.

This is not happening. There's no way Cassie is one of them.

Cassie sees her and waves from the door. Like always, she makes her way to the bar like a bull in a china shop.

Her voice rings out, several decibels higher than usual. "Hiya, Marge! Boy, do I have an earful for ya."

Likewise, she thinks, and Margie starts quaking in her shoes. Her sister is never wrong about these things.

She glances around, trying to figure out where all her saltshakers have disappeared to. Funny how things have a way of disappearing when a person really needs them. She's always had salt on hand, especially in the summer. Her customers often request it with their watermelon.

Where the hell is my salt?

Cassie sashays herself up to the bar, lighting up a cigarette. She sets down her lighter and lets out a huge sigh, blowing smoke in Margie's direction. "Whatcha looking for?"

She ignores the question, hoping to find the salt any second now. Cassie continues on with the conversation.

"You won't believe my niece. She's such a sneaky little thief."

"What happened?" Margie mumbles as she searches.

"I'm ready to kick her ass out."

"Oh, really? What has she done now?"

"She's watered down my booze, that's what she's done."

Margie finally spots the salt—directly behind her bottle of gin, for some ungodly reason. Following Mavis's instructions, she spills it in a neat line across her bar.

The move is not lost on Cassie.

"Margie, what in the Sam Hill are you doing?"

What can she say? "Well, I was reading somewhere how salt can take out stubborn stains, especially on these old bar countertops. Lord knows, I've acquired some good ones over the years. I've been wanting to try this, just always slipped my mind."

"Really? And you choose now of all times to do it?"

Margie's knees knock together. For a moment, she thinks Cassie is on to her. But the salt line doesn't seem to faze Cassie at all.

"Hell of a time to be all Suzy Homemaker, Margie."

She stares anxiously as Cassie glances around. Her eyes stop on the wall holding the phone, and Margie doesn't dare breathe.

A slow grimace crosses over Cassie's face as she stares at the wall. "That's downright disgusting!"

"What is?"

"Those walls. If you're in a cleaning mood, I'd start by scrubbing those walls down with bleach. Christ, looks like someone took a dump in their hand and threw it at the wall like some goddamn monkey!"

A few of the other patrons overhear her and start roaring with laughter.

"I'll get right on that, Cassie."

"Damn straight; the walls would probably write you a thank you note."

Margie just nods. "You don't have to be so mean about it."

"Well, maybe so." Cassie shrugs. "I better not get any of this on my clothes, though—you know what salt could do to this blouse?"

Margie says nothing, afraid what might come out of her mouth next.

"Oh, Christ!"

Now what!!

Margie's heart is about to jump out of her chest. She really wanted to punch Cassie in the face. She can't handle this kind of pressure. She ignores Cassie, as she pushes off her barstool. "Would it kill anybody to put a damn quarter in the jukebox? The thing needs a quarter in it for it to work."

"Sometimes it's nice to hear the quiet, Cassie."

She scoffs. "Yeah, well, quiet is overrated. I prefer things when they're loud. Put on some goddamn Waylon."

"Someone piss in your cereal?" one of the patrons asks.

"No, Harvey. And I wouldn't eat a bowl of that wet cardboard if you paid me a million dollars."

"I would!" someone yells across the room.

One of the regulars stands up from the bar and puts on an old Hank Williams song. "Hank's good, too," Cassie offers, sitting back down at the bar.

"I'm glad you think so, Cassie."

Margie can't help but wonder why Cassie isn't affected by the salt. Is it possible that Mavis was wrong? She'd said the salt would buy her some time, but she doesn't want to buy time; she just wants these things to go away.

She longs for the good old days when things in her town were boring. And how could one of those things get to Cassie?

Margie doesn't want trouble, but trouble always walks itself in. Her sister could give her some guidance, some assistance even, but she won't. Which irritates her to no end.

Why can't Mavis just stop in and help her?

THE FIRE

The Traveller

*J*don't know why I'm going, but I'm being led to that little dive bar on the lake, the one that looks like it was decorated by circus clowns on the inside. I feel an appealing familiarity there, and that fact somehow strengthens my resolve. I've lost hearing in my right ear, and my vision feels muted. But I just follow along this gravel road, my path to final freedom.

I hope I catch on fire. I really want to, and I don't care who sees me either; I'm done with all that. Everything that I gave a damn about died right along with my Penny. All I'm left with is an unseen rage that makes me see red wherever I go, and I don't know what to do with it. I can't hold on to it anymore; I want to let it loose and rip everything apart.

I'm not a good person to come in contact with right now.

With every step forward I can hear the sounds of the forest grow quiet. They all know about me. *Well, good.*

Nobody can hear my silent cries because I am a supreme being, and my pleas for control fall on deaf ears; I know where I am being led, and I can't fight it. And for once, my body is feeling the effects of my living here on earth. I feel strange; this is a vulnerability I haven't encountered. It makes me feel well, almost human.

As the outline of River's Edge Bar comes into view, I think to myself that liquid spirits would be good for sipping. And suddenly, I want to consume the spirits in every bottle in this place. In fact, I want to drown in them.

As I walk in, I see the normal cluster of people sitting up at the bar. But there's also an odd female presence sitting there, and I can tell right away that she's crooked. *Good. Bring it.*

I find an empty stool on the more deserted side of the bar, and everyone acknowledges me—everyone, of course, but the thing at the bar. In my mind, I can tell that she's wearing a heavy cloak. I've seen this kind of thing before, an easy way to trick the humans around her. I don't know yet how long she's been one of those things, but I'll know as soon as I get close enough.

I order a shot of whiskey. The bartender's gaze is shifty, unfocused, but she makes small talk. "How's it going?"

What a question. Laughable under the circumstances. *You want the real answer or the sugar-coated one?*

Whenever a question like that is posed, I feel the need to be polite. It is a nice way of starting a conversation, but really, do they *really* care? I'd bet that nine times out of ten, if a person were to get into the meat of what's bothering them, most people wouldn't bother sticking around to even hear it. They're too busy tuning them out before that person can spit out an entire sentence.

I ignore her question. I have a lighter in my back pocket, and I want to light myself with it, right here on this cherry-red barstool. But I hold off, the last vestiges of human decency winning out for now.

I am aware of the visual appeal of this bar, and I'd rather it not get destroyed. The whole palette seems to have been picked out by some hippie on a three-day bender. But today, I find it rather endearing.

I bring out the lighter, and start flicking it with my thumb.

The thing sitting a few seats down from me wants to play all sticky sweet. She seems unsure of me, and her demeanor remains neutral. She does seem to sense that I am a supernatural, though, and can't seem to figure out which side I am on.

Good, I'll play. I like cutting through smoke and mirrors.

The bartender tries with another question. "What brings you in, sir? I don't see you around here much."

I glare at her. I notice then that something has spooked her a great deal, and I want to tell her to stay calm, but I don't. She obviously senses the thing at the bar, too, and clearly doesn't know what to do. Normally, I would have some pity, but I'm in too much of a crap mood to summon decent feelings right now.

"Well, you wouldn't, would you?" I snipe back. "I don't venture here much. I don't like to go anywhere, really. Penny's probably been in here more than I have."

Her face lights up. "How is she?"

A stab of rage shoots through my chest with such magnitude that I almost pass out right here on this floor. I have to keep my wits about me, but I like the way she looks while talking about my love, Penny. She doesn't know what has happened to her, she is just being polite. I will answer her.

"Um, well . . ." I try and find the words, but I can't find any. Dear God in heaven, I can't handle this kind of inquiry. I close my eyes and silently pray for some strength.

I don't finish my sentence, and she continues wiping down her bar. I probably seem quite strange to her, but I'm sure she has seen her share of misfits.

I feel the tug of regret. I hate to ruin her fine establishment, but she seems smart, and I'm sure she has insurance on this place, so she will rebuild.

With every passing minute, I am more confident in what I want to do next. This surge of emotion running through me, this hate, is stronger than anything I've ever felt, and *I'm going to let it win.*

I straighten my spine.

The thing next to me is puffing hard on a cigarette, smoking it right down to the filter. She looks like she's done this many times—her face looks as tough as shoe leather. Her eyes are dodgy, and I realize she's casing the place. This erratic behavior is common in distractors.

I smelled tracings of it when I stepped inside this place.

The stool I'm sitting on is already catching fire. I don't know how it happened, but I think the lighter in my pocket must have started it, so apparently, this was meant to be.

The vinyl on this stool lights up so quickly, that I'm already starting to burn.I feel waves of it licking at the back of my legs, and spreading across my torso.

I will let myself burn.

I have not experienced this sensation before. It's nothing like when I was being punished for being on fire. This time, I can feel every scorch as it touches my skin, and I want to scream.

The thing next to me sprints for the front door. I can't quite get to it, which is unfortunate, because I want to end it right here. *She is a distractor.*

Actually, I'm surprised I couldn't get to her. Normally, I'd be right on it. *Why can't I move?*

Before I know it, the whole bar is ablaze, and the walls around me are entirely engulfed in flames. Some are even starting to collapse on themselves. Most of the people had ran out of the bar. But I just stare, mesmerized by the orange flames, and again, I feel a twinge of regret. I don't like it when bad things happen to good people, and I know the lady behind the counter to be good. I feel it in her, and in a last-minute decision, I feel myself dragging her out of the bar. She is burned quite a bit, as am I.

I hear someone screaming, and it takes me a minute to figure out that it is me. I feel different somehow, but I can't put my finger on it—I just know this isn't normal for me.

I drag her to the lake; I need to get us near the water. Once the fire on both of us is out—thanks to me rolling her into the water and dowsing us both—I notice the skin on my arms is starting to hang loose. The pain of countless stings and burns is festering all over my body. I stare at my arms, disbelieving. This has never happened to me before.

I drop down next to her, and my body screams at me. I've never experienced burning like this before, a fire that leaves me singed all over.

I hear a rustling in the reeds at the edge of the lake before I see two dogs heading my way. They both acknowledge me with a nod of their head, and I can tell the larger of the two wants to communicate.

"Your work here is not done."

"How are you talking to me?" I ask absurdly. For a moment, I think that I'm hallucinating until I remember my inherent ability to hear all things.

You're a supernatural being, remember?

Maybe the old brain is getting rusty, or maybe the shock that my body is going through has put me all out of sorts, but it's been a good stretch of time since I've communicated with an animal. Regardless, I am compelled to listen.

The dog continues. "You can do more for the people of Neelsville by staying alive."

I contemplate this. "You call this living? What a joke. I want to be with her."

"There will always be time for that."

The other dog starts talking. "You will heal like a human now. Your time as a Traveller is done. You now have an expiration."

Thank God.

"Oh, cool. Kind of like expired cereal?"

They just stare at each other. They clearly know nothing of humor.

I pose a question. "Why now, after all these thousands of years?"

"It was more than time, don't you think?" The first dog says.

The other dog speaks. "Penny intervened."

Of course she would. *Oh, my dear love, Penny. Oh God, how I love you.* "I want to be with her, let me go!"

"It is not your time. And from now on, you should be called Michael."

I let the words resonate.

The smaller of the two dogs takes over. "Someone needs to look after those wounds."

The first dog nods. "And you have unfinished business. The lives of the people here depend on it."

I glance over at the lake, and just as I do, I see one, two, and soon a half dozen other souls emerge from it. At first glance, they appear young and beautiful. But after several more appear, I see that they are all different ages. They float high above me, in this decadent, ghastly dream. They fly over to me as one, and I stare, my eyes following their every move.

Now, I've seen a great many things in this strange life of mine, but this is vastly different to behold. My eyes scan each one, taking in their expressions, memorizing every detail.

They all start to speak at once, repeating the same line, over and over.

"We all met our ends here. Please help us; please help our town. There is evil here.

I have unfinished business.

The phrase echoes in my mind as I hear Margie moaning on the ground—I don't think she can see the spirits above us—and I remember how badly she's been injured.

I have to help her.

I place my hands on the ground to push to sitting, but my entire body protests; I'm fairing no better than she is.

The dogs must have read my mind because the larger one speaks. "Your powers are not effective anymore."

I feel another presence at my side and look over.

Well, of course.

It's that spirited human I met earlier, the one riding with me in that unfortunate accident. The one that occurred just hours ago. She reminds me of a prickly cactus.

Her eyes are wide as she stares at me, then opens her mouth. "I've called an ambulance; they're on their way. Hang on, Traveller."

I want to tell her I'm not the Traveller anymore, but under the circumstances, it seems rather silly. I notice her hands shaking as she tries to caress my arm, and I realize she's doing her best to console me.

She turns to Margie and repeats what she just said. Her words sounding more unsure, and I'm wondering how Margie is fairing. *Probably not well.*

I hope the bartender can pull through this, but it doesn't look good. Hell, I hope I pull out of this.

The dogs have fallen silent; I can no longer hear their words. And suddenly, I know what I must do. I will hold on, if I can. Wait for the ambulance to arrive.

The spirits from the lake have floated off into the darkening night, and the dogs sit around us—one at our heads, the other at our feet. They feel like guardians, protecting us, and I instinctively know they will stay here until proper help arrives.

I watch the sun set itself into the lake, breathtaking colors fill the sky, and the last thing I hear is the annoying siren of the ambulance. I don't know if they've come in time, as I feel myself losing consciousness. I stare at the tall reeds as my heavy eyes flutter shut. But I can still smell the lake water, it is a comfort to me.

If I die right here on this warm ground, I know I will miss all of these things, especially the sunsets on this beautiful lake.

Of that, and only that, I am certain.

~~ The End ~~

Acknowledgements

When I first wrote, 'A Grey Resort', I never intended it to become a series. But when a dear friend said to me after reading it, 'you have to continue this story!' I started to do some research on how I wanted the story to progress. And before I knew it, the characters started taking on a life of their own, and the story practically wrote itself. This book was so easy to write, but hard to put together. I'm always incredibly grateful and humbled by the process.

I had such fun with these characters, in fact, I now frequently have inner dialogue with them (they won't leave me alone). ☺ I'm always mystified and in awe of the whole writing process, and I've met such amazing and creative people along the way. My path to becoming an author was not an easy one. But like everything else, I take it one day at a time, and still do.

I'd like to thank Melissa Frey for her great advice about the book, I'm so appreciative. I'd also like to thank Randi Brower for her wonderful enthusiasm and input. I'd like to acknowledge Kyle Jennings for his inspiration. I hope you know that your music means so much to so many people. I'm so grateful that you listened to your dad when he said, 'stay the course.'

I'd like to thank my friends for cheering me on, and giving me that extra incentive to continue on with the series. Much thanks to my friend, Jennifer Lonnberg, for giving me the courage to write it my way.

I'd like to thank my husband for taking the reins in the household when need be. You are my rock, and I can't thank you enough. Thank you to all my family, friends, and fans for helping to keep this dream alive.

I'm so grateful to my parents for giving my sister and I the most amazing experience while growing up on that mystical lake, oh so long ago. These memories I hold dear, and I know the people that have stayed there feel the same.

~~Long live pontoon boat rides, fishing at dusk, PBR, and endless hours of walks through the woods, these memories I will keep in my heart forever.~~